SECRET SANTA 2: A CHRISTMAS TO REMEMBER

Secret Santa Series

Book 2

KAY LYONS

Kindred Spirits Publishing

Introduction

Hello Readers!

If you're a fan of my writing, you know the Secret Santa series is a little different from my "normal" work. But that's what Christmas is all about, isn't it? Believing in what isn't seen?

After Holly's story was published in **Secret Santa,** I received numerous emails asking for Devon to get his happy ending. Well, let me know what you think!

I love hearing from my readers. You can contact me through my website at Kay Lyons, Author or at kay@ kaylyonsauthor.com.

Enjoy Devon and Kelsey's story!

God bless,

Kay

____

Chapter 1

____

"Not again," Devon Sage muttered to himself when he heard a familiar whistle echo off the tunnel walls.

Devon quickened his steps to head off the old man before he managed to get any deeper into the tunnel system leading to Yorkton, the secret underground city located beneath New York City.

Like a scene from a Hollywood movie set, a Vegas casino, or super-secret government substation only the president and a select few cabinet members were aware of, Yorkton was state-of-the-art. The ceiling of the city held a computer-operated sun, moon, and stars, which changed on schedule. The air filtration system fed them fresher air than what could be found in the city above, and everyone walked or bicycled to their various jobs within the organization so pollution was kept to a minimum. Still, after living in Alaska most of his life, he wasn't sure the move to Yorkton had been a wise one. A fake city, even with all of it's fancied high-techness, was still fake, and he missed the wide-open space of the Alaskan bush.

Devon rounded the curve and planted himself in the center of the underground passageway, hands on his hips, as he waited for the old guy to look up and see him.

If the homeless man made it into the inner tunnels, from there, he could be a much larger problem because they used those systems to transport their goods out of Yorkton to a shipping warehouse.

"Oh. Ah... hello there, young man."

Devon couldn't help but shake his head. "Wally, how many times have I told you? You can't be down here."

Wally lifted his hand and scratched his balding head through the knit cap he wore.

"Oh, it's all right. I'm looking for something."

"Uh huh. Come on. Turn around and go back."

"But I have to find my dog."

"You don't have a dog."

"I do so have a dog. Name's Bronte. Have you seen her?"

The man made a show of looking around Devon to the semi-lit tunnel behind him. He even whistled but then ruined the attempt to deceive by shooting a glance at Devon, as though to check whether or not Devon bought the act. He didn't.

Wally always had a story of some sort. But like all of the other reasons Wally gave for being down in the tunnels, Devon didn't believe "Bronte" existed. More troubling was the fact the man's visits had become more frequent. Each time, Wally managed to get a little deeper into the off-limits area before getting caught.

It made sense that Wally sought protection away from the dangers outside the alley grates and subway lines, where the warmth of the underground drifted to where the transient sought shelter from the elements. Who wouldn't take advantage of what little heat there was to be found? Better yet, go underground where few dared to venture, since that in itself was a form of safety.

Devon blocked Wally's way once again when the old man tried to continue by. "No, I haven't seen a dog. Now turn around and leave before you get hurt. I've told you, it isn't safe down here. There's a reason the tunnels are off-limits to the public."

Wally rubbed his hands together and lifted them to his mouth to blow on them.

"I haven't seen any danger. Not even one of those giant gators people say roam around down here. Kind of wish I would stumble upon one of them. Bet they'd make for some good eating."

Devon barely caught himself before he smiled at the man's statement. The rumors about massive alligators, and rats, and even vampires had been started by the Lowlanders as a way of keeping the Highlanders from trespassing below ground. The stories worked for the most part, especially given the creepiness of the under-ground, but then there were always some--like Wally-- who were determined to explore the tunnels no matter what.

"I'm not doing any harm, son. Just trying to stay warm. Can't blame a man for that, can you?"

Wally's statement hit home and Devon struggled to remember the rules of the Elder Council versus the empathy he felt for the old man. "I don't blame you for seeking shelter from the cold, but the fact remains that it can't be down here."

"Bah! It can't be that bad. You're down here. Besides, you know me. I'm not going to get into something I shouldn't. Can't you let an old man be, Devon?"

Devon winced. He shouldn't have told the man his real name. "Wally...."

"It's winter, son. It's so cold it makes a man's bones shake. Wouldn't hurt anything to let me stay. At least let me warm up. Don't throw me out into the snow."

Devon frowned at the man's words, hating that he had to be the bad guy. Winter in New York was brutal, especially for a man Wally's age. And the arrival of sleet and snow made the cold that much worse. "Rules are rules. I'll lose my job if I let you stay."

"Surely not. Tell me who you work for because I'll tell them--"

"Wally, stop arguing for the sake of arguing."

"Just stating facts. That a crime?"

Devon fought his frustration and wished he could do more for the homeless man. Wally was harmless but the restrictions--the laws of the Elder Council-- were in place for a reason.

"You know, you could give me a job and then I wouldn't be trespassing. Say, that's a right fine idea." Wally straightened a bit and made a show of smoothing the front of his dirty coat. "You can just hire me right now. I'll help you guard the tunnels. Where do we need to go next?"

"*You* need to leave. Look, Wally, I'm sorry. I know it's warmer here than up above, but you've got to go. Find a shelter and get on a list before all the beds are taken."

"I don't like those places. I've told you over and over that I don't."

Devon didn't like the thought of sending the elderly man to a shelter where his age might make him a target of unsavory people, but it couldn't be helped. "I know you don't, but it's better than being cold, right? They can help you where I can't. Now let's go."

Devon waited for Wally to turn and retrace his steps. Wally muttered something under his breath; head hanging low as he reluctantly complied.

Devon tried and failed to ignore the man's slumped shoulders and downtrodden body language, and reminded himself of the bigger picture.

Yorkton had a large security patrol stationed throughout the outer rims to keep outsiders from getting too close to those tunnels used daily by the underground city. The homeless, runaways, stray animals—at some point they all sought shelter underground when the weather turned cold. "If I see Bronte I'll bring her to you."

"What? Oh, oh, yeah. Yeah, you do that. She's a good dog."

Devon smothered a laugh at the old man's response. If Wally had brought a dog into the tunnels, Devon would be highly surprised.

Once they reached an area close to an entrance/exit point, Devon stopped. "Can you find your way out from here?"

"Of course," Wally said, tugging on his cap so that it covered the top of his ears. "I'm old, not crazy."

Despite the dim light, Devon noticed how red and chapped the man's hands were. He removed his gloves, holding them out to Wally. "Take these. You need them more than I do."

Wally accepted the gloves but hesitated in putting them on.

"Why... these look special. Almost…handmade?"

Devon smiled at the man's observation and nodded. "They are." When it was obvious Wally wanted more information, Devon inhaled and sighed. "My mother made them."

"She did a right fine job. But, son, I can't--"

"You can. Don't worry. I have at least three more pair. They'll keep you warm. Take these. I won't miss them."

Wally stared down at the gloves, running his chapped fingertips over a finely sewn seam.

"Seeing as that's the case, then..." Wally slipped on the gloves. "You're right. I'm warmer already," the man murmured with a slight nod of his head. "Haven't seen anything made this special in a long, long time. You sure you want to give'em up? It's pretty chilly back in those tunnels. Nothing like being thrown out into the cold, of course," Wally added with a pointed stare, as though to shame Devon into acquiescing, "but cold all the same."

Devon dug into his coat pocket and retrieved a couple of the protein bars he kept on hand for just such run-ins. Wally had lost quite a bit of weight in the short time Devon had known him and he now carried the snacks and water because he couldn't stand the thought of the old man being hungry. "Here. Take these. "

"Thank you, son. The other workers never offer anything."

Because it was against the rules. Feed a stray and it would stay.

He wasn't supposed to give Highlanders food, shelter, or anything else that might draw unwanted attention to his presence or who he worked for. Usually, Devon stuck to the rule, but... there was just something about Wally. Something that wouldn't allow Devon to turn the old man completely away.

Devon couldn't imagine being homeless at Wally's age, much less alone, hungry, and cold. But that was the very reason to so vigilantly protect the community hidden beneath the city's streets. To keep Yorkton from being discovered so that men like Wally would be cared for--via the proper channels.

This time last year Holly Klaas had broken the rules to save a pilot who'd crashed into the Alaskan bush during a sudden snowstorm.

He'd given her an extremely hard time then about bringing the man into their secret compound—Alaska's version of Yorkton—but here he was a year later, going against the rules to feed an old man and help keep him warm. He'd be a hypocrite not to acknowledge the fact that he'd broken the same rule Holly had.

He owed Holly an apology but to give it now would mean swallowing his pride and he wasn't quite sure he was ready to do that just yet. So maybe instead, a kind gesture to honor Holly's decision would have to do.

Devon clapped Wally on the back to urge him on his way. "Keep your head down and stay safe. And if you won't go to the shelter," he said, lowering his voice in case his voice echoed off the tunnel walls to those near the tunnel's exit, "stick close outside and stay put. That's better than nothing."

"I'd be a might warmer if you'd let me stay back

there." Wally tilted his head to the darkness from which they'd come.

Devon shook his head and lowered his voice even more. "I could lose my job if my bosses find out I've helped you at all. Now go. I've got to get back to my patrol."

"Patrol? Is that what you are? A cop?"

Caught by his choice of words, Devon hesitated. "Security."

"For who?"

"Not important. Now stop stalling."

The old man must have sensed Devon had reached the end of his patience because Wally nodded and slowly ambled off, opening one of the protein bars with a rattle of the packaging.

Devon watched, waiting until Wally shuffled his way toward the grate leading to one of New York's many alleys. The faint hint of streetlights fell on Wally's grizzled features and Devon stared, struck by the difference in the old man just in the last few months since finding him the first time.

Devon made a mental note to see what programs were available to aid the old man. Wally might not want to go, but surely if the red tape was done for him, he'd accept the help for the winter months, if nothing else?

Devon pondered the question and watched to make sure Wally exited the passage and that he didn't sneak back inside.

He'd turned to go when he heard muffled voices outside the grate. Devon winced, guessing Wally had been spotted. It was going to be a long night if the pattern repeated itself and others tried to gain access through the grate.

Devon quietly made his way closer to the exit to head off any potential curiosity. That's when he heard curses and grunts and the sounds of a scuffle.

"Give it up, old man."

"I told you..." Wally wheezed, trying to catch his breath. "I don't have. Anything."

Devon fisted his hands, forbidden to leave the underground or interfere. But when a punch left Wally doubled over and crying out in pain, Devon reacted. He didn't allow himself to think of the consequences as he pushed open the grate as quietly as possible and slipped through unnoticed, thanks to the attackers' distraction.

"Yeah, well we know you do. Man, I *told* you," the thug said to his partner. "We done hit the lottery."

Every rule and warning ever issued to the security teams responsible for safety flashed through Devon's brain at the speed of light, but he still found himself above-ground for the first time since joining Yorkton's guard after leaving Alaska. The smell of garbage assaulted him along with the noise of the nearby busy street. "Let him go."

Both men turned to stare at Devon but neither of the thugs turned loose of the old man.

"Ah, man, what?" one of the men said, surprise sharpening his tone. "What's you and Mr. Moneybags doing in there, eh?" The thug looked at Devon with a sneer. "How much he pay you? Cause old man's gonna pay us now. Oh, yeah, he is."

The smaller of the thugs laughed as he held a sagging Wally upright with his arms trapped behind his back. Devon lunged toward the larger of the men, a lightning strike of fear-laced adrenaline surging through

him when the thug pulled a gun just as Devon took him
to the icy ground.

Chapter 2

JT Wallingford: From Billionaire to Homeless?

Kelsey Richards stared at the tabloid headline and the picture of her grandfather dressed in rags and looking like he'd slept in a dumpster.

But it was him, no doubt about it.

"Well? Please tell me my eyes are deceiving me," Kelsey's bookstore assistant manager said, a note of trepidation in her voice. "Kels, *is* it him?"

Kelsey blinked, unable to take her eyes off the photo as she nodded. "I'm...yeah. It's him."

"Oh, wow. I'm so sorry. I know you said he's been acting a little strange lately but I had *no* idea..."

Neither did Kelsey.

"The article says money certainly isn't the issue. So nice of them to check into his financials before printing," Amanda added with disgust. "So why does he do it? Better yet, what are you going to do?"

Kelsey tore her gaze away from the photo and lowered the tabloid to the counter in front of her. "I'm not sure." What was JT thinking? Why on earth would he do such a thing? A man his age and in his state of health. He'd survived pneumonia and bronchitis and still had breathing issues for which he received regular medical care. Why on earth would he go out in the bitter cold of night to rummage around dank alleys and dumpsters, pretending to be *homeless*?

"Well, you're going to have to do something," Amanda said. "I mean, seriously, Kels, he's old and filthy rich. He can't go out walking the streets alone. And after that article, every idiot in New York City will be looking for him just hoping to score some cash or to *kidnap* him. You know how crazy people can be."

Kelsey wanted to scoff at the thought of someone going as far as to kidnap her grandfather but the world *had* gone crazy and, truth be told, kidnapping was a legitimate possibility. People did unimaginable things where money was concerned. And, by publishing the article, the tabloid had painted a big, red target with a dollar sign on her grandfather's very wealthy back.

Over the next few minutes, Kelsey rushed her employees through the closing routine and locked up her indie bookstore, with no time to take in the beauty of the historic building, with its grand wooden bookshelves and ornate, hand-carved staircase leading to the upper level. Instead of a sanctuary from the world, the much loved bookstore was a problem that had to be dealt with before she could go tackle the other, bigger, problem of confronting JT. "Amanda, are you finished?"

"Yeah, everything is ready for tomorrow. We're good to go for the night."

The last of the employees to leave the building, Amanda led the way to the exit, drawing Bronte's attention. Kelsey's standard-size Labradoodle opened her sleepy eyes and regarded them from the giant dog bed. Bronte rolled to her feet when she spotted Amanda with her purse, a sure sign it was time to go home. After a yawn, stretch, and shake of her wild curls, the poodle mix quickly moved to Kelsey's side for some love. "Hey, girlie. Are you ready to go home?"

Home was literally above her head and a short elevator ride away through the many floors being renovated, but first she had to lock up and set the alarm once Amanda left the building.

Kelsey waved goodbye to her assistant manager before she hit the security system and lights, and made her way to the back of the store. Bronte's nails clicked rapidly on the wood floors beside of Kelsey and the sweet Doodle must have sensed Kelsey's urgency because the dog didn't pause to sniff out the many scents carried in by their customers off New York's streets.

Please be home, JT. Be home. You seriously can't be doing this. Really?

Swiping her keycard and punching the private elevator button did nothing to ease her anxiety, but the rapid jabbing gave her something to focus on other than fear. Finally the doors opened and she entered the extra security code that would take her to the penthouse.

The thirty-two second ascent seemed to take a thousand times longer than it normally did and Kelsey squeezed through the elevator doors the moment they opened. "JT? Hello? JT, are you home?"

A rapid, thorough check of the apartment made it clear JT was nowhere to be found. Again.

Kelsey rushed back to the purse she'd tossed aside at the entry and found her phone. Unlike her own aversion to technology, JT seemed to favor the latest gadgets and always had his cell near him.

Except... if he did have it on him, why wasn't he answering? Voicemail had never been more frustrating. "JT, it's me. I'm worried. Where are you? Call me as soon as you get this. I mean it. Please, call me. It's urgent."

For the past several weeks JT had been acting odder than usual, distracted and focused on something, and he was unwilling to share. He'd been coming in late or not coming home until the following morning, usually meeting Kelsey somewhere along the way as she made her way downstairs to open the bookstore.

Since JT had spent most of his life as a workaholic she hadn't given much thought to his whereabouts, knowing full well most business deals were conducted over boring dinners and in private club libraries over aged brandy and cigars. She'd also considered the fact JT might have a lady friend. Grandma, or Gram as Kelsey called her, had passed away ten years ago so a companion wasn't entirely out of the question.

But dressing up as a homeless man? "JT, where are you? What are you doing besides making it impossible for me to not worry?"

Perhaps he'd been approached by a theater company, yet again, to take a part in a play? JT was well known for his boisterous voice and big character. A year ago, he'd been asked by a friend of a friend of an off-Broadway production to play the part of Santa Claus. JT had been too busy at the time, but he'd made it clear he'd considered the asking to be quite the honor.

Could that be what he's doing? Was he practicing for a part?

Of what? A homeless Santa? Get real, Kels.

No, he would've told her. There was no reason to keep that a secret from her.

Kelsey paced the floor of the penthouse apartment, her stomach growling from hunger but her appetite iffy. After following Kelsey the first few laps across the glossy floor, Bronte hopped up onto the couch, stared at Kelsey and yawned.

"Yeah, well, I'm tired too," Kelsey grumbled, watching Bronte lower her head atop her front paws and blink slowly. Bronte tipped the adorability scale, looking like one of those soft, furry stuffies from the children's section on the second floor of the bookstore. "I guess one of us should sleep. Might as well be you since I know it won't be me."

Bronte yawned again and Kelsey did the only thing she could do—pace and pray.

Five minutes later, Kelsey had changed into comfortable leggings and an oversized sweater and prepared herself to wait for JT's return. She glanced at her fitness watch and noted the massive number of steps she'd taken during the day. But after a twelve-hour shift at the bookstore, plus the hours before and after working, her body ached to curl up with Bronte and relax, not wear a path on the apartment floor from fret and worry about JT.

Especially when he was fine. He hadn't been kidnapped. How silly was that? He was just out. With a friend.

At a meeting.

That was running late.

Too busy to answer his phone.

She was not worried. Not at all.

Her stomach growled noisily.

Unable to deny her hunger, she veered from her pacing to go to the kitchen. Thankfully, Rita had been in today and the fridge was stocked with two different soups, a casserole, and several other dishes, plus a pan of lasagna, all ready to heat and eat. Rita was the only reason Kelsey didn't have delivery on a nightly basis.

Kelsey grabbed the lasagna and quickly warmed a piece, wolfing it down in her anxiousness while mindlessly pacing the kitchen. She washed her plate and fork, wiped down the sink, and back to pacing she went, stopping only to look out at the skyline.

It was getting late. Really late for an old man who was usually in bed before she closed at ten.

Should she call the police? But what could they do? It wasn't like JT was actually missing... was he?

JT, where are you? What are you doing out there? Come home!

Kelsey called JT's cell phone again but hung up when it went straight to voicemail. When JT checked his phone he would see all her missed calls.

She moved back to the entry table where she'd dropped her bag and pulled out the tabloid once more, studying the photo. Maybe if she could figure out where the photo had been taken... or maybe she should call the paper and find out from the reporter?

It's pushing midnight.

A loud ring pierced the air and startled Kelsey. Her pulse pounded in her throat and she dropped the paper and ignored its messy slide across the floor from the breeze she created rushing to answer her phone. "JT? H-hello? JT?"

"Ms. Richards?"

She pressed her trembling fingers to her aching forehead and rubbed hard. "Yes. This is Kelsey Richards. Who is this?"

"My name is Nurse Borjeski from Central Hospital. I'm calling about your grandfather.... I'm afraid I have bad news."

Chapter 3

Kelsey rushed out the door to the hospital, desperate to get to her grandfather, praying all the while that he was all right.

The nurse who had called hadn't known the details of JT's condition, only that he had been injured in a mugging and required medical assistance. Thankfully his emergency contact information had been stored in his phone.

The taxi's tires squealed to a stop outside of the emergency room entrance and Kelsey shoved several bunched bills through the slot, thanking the man for his speedy delivery, with a rushed murmur and the promised generous tip.

She fought her impatience and barely managed to keep from barreling over the couple in front of her, who seemed bent on slowing her down as they argued over who had to call Aunt Vee and tell her Jimmy had OD'd again.

A tired looking woman on a phone call was at the admittance desk and held up a hand to still Kelsey's inquiry before it spilled out. Kelsey looked around for someone else to help her, but the area was devoid of staff and overflowing with potential patients and their companions. Most of these people looked irritated that she might slow their progression through the tangle of red tape.

Finally, the thirty-something tired looking woman ended the call and typed painfully slow into the computer in front of her before making eye contact with Kelsey.

"Can I help you?"

"Yes, my grandfather. Someone called and said he'd been injured during a mugging."

"Patient's name?"

Kelsey lowered her voice. "JT Wallingford."

That got the woman's attention. She immediately stood.

"I'm so sorry for the delay. We've been waiting for you to arrive."

If she wasn't in such a hurry to find JT and learn of his injuries, Kelsey would've laughed at the woman's about-face. Obviously the hospital's higher-ups had informed the staff to be on the lookout for Kelsey, and the sudden change in attitude showed the power of JT's name. That was because there was a wing in nearly every hospital in the city with the Wallingford name attached to it. This one was no exception. "Where is he?"

"This way. I'll show you. A room is being prepared for him but he's still in the ER for now."

Kelsey followed the woman down the hall past curtained rooms and beeping monitors. Low murmurs could be heard coming from the other side of the curtains and more than one of the visitors who waited in a bedside chair made eye contact with Kelsey as she walked by.

She couldn't help but wonder if she wore the same tired, stressed expression as they did. How could she not? "He has to be admitted? He was hurt that badly?"

"Yes, I'm afraid so. The doctor will explain."

The woman's words did nothing to reassure Kelsey of her grandfather's condition so the knot in her stomach grew. JT was her only living relative and she absolutely couldn't bear the thought of losing him. Especially not to something as senseless as a mugging.

She had to get through to him and convince him to stop whatever drove him to behave in such a manner.

The woman from the front desk finally paused at the end of the ER cubicles and knocked discreetly on the divider between the rooms before pushing back the curtain. Kelsey only had eyes for JT, who lay in the bed looking older than his seventy-eight years and much too fragile.

His lower lip was swollen to twice its normal size. The darkness of a still-forming bruise shadowed his mouth before it disappeared into his silvery-white beard. He had a small cut on his left cheek under his eye, and blood stains on his hands. But most worrisome was his expression, strained with pain and weariness and... defeat? "Poppy?"

She rarely called her grandfather anything other than his initials, but looking at him now...

JT's lashes fluttered open and he managed a smile, though the effort caused a wince that ripped her insides in half.

"Don't look so frightened, my girl. I'm fine. I told

them not to call you but obviously someone didn't listen. I should be going home shortly. You shouldn't have bothered with me."

Kelsey rushed to his side and carefully hugged him before she straightened and grasped one of his hands in hers. Where had all of the blood come from? She searched what she could see of his face, arms, and hands, and saw a few scrapes but nothing to warrant the amount of blood staining his skin. "You're not a bother. And you're not going anywhere. Not until you've been checked over thoroughly and I know you're okay."

"I'm fine, my dear."

"You're not *fine*," she said, taking his hand in hers and lifting it, so that he could see what she saw.

"The blood? That doesn't belong to me, sweetheart. It's Devon's. He bled so much. I couldn't get it to stop."

Devon? Devon who? She opened her mouth to ask when she realized they weren't alone in the cubicle. A white-coated man turned and Kelsey froze when recognition dawned. *Nooo. Not now!*

"It's good to see you again, Kelsey."

A flash of pain zapped through her, her nerves tingling as though burning. Kelsey took a step back. She wanted to get away from the man who'd taken her heart and then shattered it for the entire world to see and gossip about. *Yet another reason to hate the tabloids.* "Neil. I didn't see you."

"That's understandable given the circumstances."

Her former fiancée looked as handsome as ever in his perfectly pressed doctor coat and dark blue scrubs, a stethoscope hanging around his neck like a beacon to draw even more attention to an already striking image. Tall, blond, and handsome, Neil was the stereotypical physician as portrayed on television dramas. The kind that garnered sexy nicknames and viral fandom.

The rollercoaster of breakup emotions blasted through Kelsey's brain and she hated herself for being so weak and distracted. Yes, she was even a little bitter, during a time when she needed to be strong and focused.

Nothing mattered now but JT. Period.

But right now she wanted to use that stethoscope to check to see if Neil had a heart at all. She simply couldn't imagine doing to him, or anyone, what he'd done to her.

"If you need anything, doctor, I'll be at my desk," the woman said, eyeing Neil with a flirtatious smile as she passed.

Kelsey watched the interplay with disgust. As they'd made their way through the hall she thought the woman was lackluster or worn down, but with a handsome doctor around, she perked right up.

Amazing how that happens.

The moment the woman was gone, Kelsey lifted her chin and forced herself to get a grip. Neil and his tabloid-worthy flirtations were no longer her concern. She'd take a long night with a good book over a cheating man any day of the week. Maybe some women would allow Neil's looks and bank account to sway their acceptance of betrayal and infidelity, but she wasn't one of them. "What are you doing here?"

"I'm the head neurologist."

"He has a head wound?" She visibly searched JT for signs of injury and smoothed her fingers gently over her grandfather's grizzled head. No bumps, bruises or blood that she could see.

"Not exactly. JT doesn't present any signs of head trauma but he was extremely confused at the scene and while being brought in. I've ordered tests in order to obtain a better picture as to the cause."

"I see." She smoothed her fingertips over JT's age-gnarled hand, unable to let go. "Any other injuries?"

"JT has a hairline fracture in a rib but nothing appears to be outright broken," Neil said. "He'll be sore for quite a while, though, and will need monitoring and rest. Our biggest concern is the potential for pneumonia, especially given his recent medical issues."

His ribs? His heart? If those were the concerns, why weren't the heads of orthopedics and cardiovascular here? She glanced at her ex-fiancé once more but immediately looked away. There was only so much she could handle of Neil under the circumstances. Shifting her attention to her grandfather, she focused on what he'd said upon her arrival. "Who is this Devon person you mentioned?"

"JT's rescuer," Neil informed her. "Devon was brought in with a gunshot wound."

Gunshot? "How bad is it? Has his family been contacted? Will he be okay?"

"He's stable. It was a graze so no surgery needed. They're working on the rest."

She shook her head, trying without success to clear the worry and fog of fatigue after a long day and what apparently was going to be an even longer night. "JT, are you in pain? Can I get you anything?"

"I'm fine," JT insisted with a squeeze to her fingers. "Stop worrying, my dear."

"I'll stop worrying after the tests," Kelsey murmured. "Maybe. But I have to know you're okay first."

"She's right. Needless to say we're going to sort this out, JT. The scans I've ordered will help shed some light on what's going on. The best thing for you to do is rest until the orderlies come to transport you."

Neil stepped closer to the bed, invading her personal space.

"Kelsey, can we talk?"

Maybe it was childish of her but her stomach knotted at the mere mention of being alone with him. " I need to be here, to go with JT when they take him for tests."

"MRI is backed up and he's not critical. It will be a little while."

"Surely whatever it is can wait. I want to stay with JT." The last thing she wanted was to spend any more time with Neil than was absolutely necessary. Thankfully JT provided the perfect excuse.

JT patted the hand she gripped so tightly. She drew strength from his touch and hoped JT felt the same. Her grandfather didn't like being fussed over but he would have to get used to it. The thought of him hurt, out there alone... The thought of losing him... She just couldn't....

"I'm fine, my dear. I *am*. I took a few blows, that's all. Just enough to bruise my old ego and remind me that I'm not as young as I'd like to think. Don't look so worried."

Neil set aside the computer tablet he held and gave them his full attention.

"She has reason to be concerned, JT. This could've ended much worse than it did. You're lucky to be alive."

Not lucky. *Blessed.* When a man of JT's age managed to survive an armed robbery with minor injuries, it was pretty obvious JT had a special purpose. Everyone did. But Neil would roll his eyes if she voiced her opinion out loud, and give her that look of his that dismissed her beliefs without actually saying so. Neil needed no God. Who needed God when Neil had a God complex the size of New York City in his life?

Stop! You're letting his presence get into your head. Just breathe. "Neil, why are you here? Surely there were other doctors on duty?"

Chapter 4

Neil shifted his weight from foot to foot and gave her a look that indicated she'd insulted him with her comment. But, seriously, what were the odds that the head of neurology just happened to be working when JT was injured?

"The hospital administrator contacted me because of our relationship."

"Former relationship." Okay, so she'd had to say it. *Had* to.

"And the hospital board personally asked me to oversee JT's case due to his recent behavior."

"Neil thinks I'm crazy just because I decided to exchange my tailored suits for something a little less showy," JT muttered.

Kelsey glanced down at her grandfather and found his eyes closed but he'd obviously been listening to every word. Watching him, JT opened his eyes and sent Neil a silencing glare.

JT knew how heartbroken she'd been after Neil's betrayal and his expression made it clear he wasn't pleased by Neil's presence anymore than she was. Some people in her grandfather's position would've taken advantage of his power and position with the hospital and made it clear Neil was no longer welcome to practice medicine there. With JT's money, he could've kept Neil from getting hired anywhere in the city, the country, thereby ruining Neil's career. But not JT. Neil was a good doctor, and JT would never destroy someone's life's work to satisfy a personal vendetta.

"As is the hospital board, I'm extremely concerned," Neil said to JT. "Kelsey, has JT had any other episodes? Shown other signs of unusual or abnormal behavior?"

"Episodes?" she repeated, at a loss until she remembered the article. She'd had no idea of JT's wanderings.

"I'll show you an *episode*, you ungrateful--"

"Stop," she said, squeezing JT's hand as though that alone would calm him. "Or you'll make things worse. *Poppy*. Look at me."

JT set his mouth in a deep frown and glared at Neil but managed to quiet down at her warning.

"JT, this is important. Have there been any other incidents?" Neil pressed. He indicated a pile of clothing nearby before reaching into his pristine coat pocket to pull out a folded piece of paper. Neil handed it to JT. "Given that photo and article, it's obvious tonight wasn't the first time you've gone out there like that. Were you aware of what you were doing? How long have you exhibited this change in behavior? When did it begin?" When JT didn't respond, Neil turned to her. "Kelsey?"

She wasn't sure what to say in regard to JT's sudden penchant for pretending to be homeless, but until she talked to JT one-on-one she certainly wasn't going to jump on Neil's references to episodes or incidents, or side with her ex about anything. "Neil, what are you trying to imply?"

"I told you," JT grumbled, crumpling the paper in his hand. "Neil thinks I'm crazy. Truth is, any man worth his salt knows *crazy* is chasing easy women when they're already engaged to a woman of worth." Her grandfather proceeded to cock one eye open in a lopsided squint resembling Popeye's, his expression a clear sign of being upset.

"For once, JT, we agree," Neil murmured. "That's why I've reached out to Kelsey so many times, but she's refused to see me or hear my side of things."

"I told you I needed time." The words came spilling out before she could stop them. She was *not* going to get drawn into this argument here and now. "Neil, I'd like to speak to JT alone."

Her grandfather shifted sideways and squirmed in the hospital bed, looking as though he attempted to settle himself more comfortably. With bruised ribs, however, she doubted he would find much comfort.

"Sweetheart, just because I've been doing something out of the ordinary for someone of my age and status does *not* mean I've lost my mind. The vultures are just circling and looking for a way to attack."

"I'm no vulture, JT. I'm trying to help you." Neil's tone revealed his growing frustration.

"Mmm-hmm. That's what they all say."

"I'm looking out for your health and well-being," Neil said, hands planted on his hips. "As well as Kelsey's. Isn't she more important than your pride?"

"Bah. I'm old and people are trying to take advantage because that's the way it's done in this world. But if you truly cared for Kelsey, you'd have considered the consequences before *you* had an episode, now, wouldn't you?"

"*Enough.*" Kelsey felt a humiliated flush rising from her chest into her cheeks, unable to stop the rush of pain that came with it. She couldn't *do this* now, and it was time to get them all back on track. "JT, you know I don't believe you're crazy, but your actions do beg the question of why? And you might as well answer the question in front of Neil because it'll save you *and* me the trouble of repeating your response. What is going on? How many times have you gone out there like that and put yourself in danger?"

"Or others?" Neil pressed. "Because maybe you got by with it and nothing has happened until tonight, but that man, Devon, was injured saving you. You can't ignore that. And you'll be extremely lucky if he doesn't sue."

Leave it to Neil to worry about such things at a time like this. Maybe it was a practical thought to some, but to her it wasn't a priority. Given JT's wealth, yeah, this Devon person probably would sue, but right now she was just grateful he'd saved JT. Wasn't that all that mattered?

"Look, JT, we've discussed security before. The danger to you and those around you is real because of who you are. You could've easily been the one shot tonight and it could've been much worse than the grazing head wound Devon suffered."

JT gently tugged on her hand. She followed his urging and leaned over the hospital bed so that he could whisper to her.

"I am sorry, my dear. I in no way meant to cause you distress or anyone harm."

She stared into her grandfather's tired blue eyes and bruised face. "I know you didn't. Just don't do it again. Please?"

JT didn't respond to her request and in that moment she knew there was a battle ahead of them. But why? *Why* was he behaving like this?

"Devon took care of me, protected me, and we must take care of him. His bills and expenses. See to it for me. Would you, my dear?"

She agreed without hesitation. "Of course. Though I'll need more information. I don't recall you mentioning a Devon before."

JT shut his eyes a moment, his head making a rasping sound on the pillow behind him.

"He's a friend," JT murmured. "Make sure he lacks for nothing. And I want to talk to him. Make sure I'm told when he's awake so I can speak to him."

"Okay," she said, not at all surprised by her grandfather's request or his generosity. JT had made his fortune in a time when the world was still kind and men were honorable. It was only right to help the man who'd rescued him.

What did concern her? JT's intensity. What was so urgent that he had to speak to the man when they were both currently lying in hospital beds? She got the distinct impression JT wasn't being completely forthcoming in his answers or relationship with Devon. Was JT's hesitancy because of Neil's presence in the room?

"No worries." Kelsey straightened up after placing a gentle kiss on her grandfather's wrinkled cheek. "You get some rest, all right? The tests will probably take most of the night so you need to sleep while you can. I'll go

check on your friend and settle the financial arrangements. I'll be back in a few minutes."

"Thank you, my dear. I think I will close my eyes for
a bit. All of the excitement has made me a bit puny."

He'd held most of the conversion with his eyes
closed, an obvious sign of his exhaustion. She brushed
her fingertips over his shoulder, willing him strength and
healing.

Men like her grandfather didn't handle growing old
well. And why should they? After conquering Wall
Street, or in JT's case, the publishing world during its
heyday--having his body and mind fail him wasn't something he could merely accept. Men of power wanted to
remain in power. It was their adrenaline fix.

She squeezed JT's hand one last time before she
reluctantly let go and moved toward the door. As she'd
feared he would, Neil fell into step behind her. When
she turned to go back toward the desk to take care of
Devon's medical expenses, Neil snagged her arm.

"This way."

She glanced up at him, not in the mood to be forced
into a conversation she didn't want to have here of all
places, but Neil's expression related the seriousness of
the moment.

"We need to talk about JT and the hospital board."

Hearing that, Kelsey allowed Neil to guide her
further down the opposite hall, noting that he drew the
attention of every female he passed.

At one time the sight wouldn't have bothered her.
She lived in a city full of beautiful things, people
included, and it was only natural for those things to be
noticed and admired. But now... Now she wondered if
one of the women they met along the corridor was *the*

half-naked woman depicted in the compromising tabloid photos with Neil that had ended their engagement. Or perhaps a one-night stand she knew nothing about?

Kelsey slowed her steps as she tried to prepare herself for a private conversation with the man who had been the final straw when it came to men. During her awkward teen years she'd earned the flattering attentions of pretty boys at school. Boys who'd been trained from birth to network their way into valuable connections for later in life and saw her as a conduit to getting on JT's radar.

College boys were much the same, though, wilder and more blatant about their desires for power, money, and sex. Still, JT's wealth and her connection to him inevitably came to the forefront due to requests for introductions, backing, or support for some project or another.

And then Neil...

He'd romanced her. Just like in the novels she liked to read. Flowers, dinners, gifts. All the right words and all the right moves. Why did all men say they weren't "that guy" and then turn into the very thing they vowed they'd never be?

Spying an on call room up ahead of them, she dug in her heels. "Neil, okay. This is far enough. What did you want to tell me about the board?"

Bad enough to have to communicate with Neil when she didn't want to, but she wasn't about to allow him to take her into a private room where she was fairly certain he would try to charm her into the second chance he wanted. He had to behave himself in the corridor.

Neil must have sensed she wasn't going to take another step because he gently tugged her to one side of the wide hall and looked around them as though about to share national secrets.

Unlike the area near the ER, this space was surprisingly quiet and calm, with only one other person at the far end staring at a computer screen located atop a rolling cart.

Neil leaned his broad shoulder against the wall and crossed one foot in front of the other, the pose casual and yet purposeful. He *knew* he was good-looking and charismatic and he wasn't above using his appearance to his advantage, to disarm and set at ease. Infatuate. Smile and tease and tempt until the barriers lowered.

How funny that she could now identify the poses for what they were, but how easily she'd fallen for them before learning the truth?

"I've missed you. It really is good to see you again, Kelsey. I've wanted so badly to talk to you but... When you wouldn't return my calls or see me, I thought maybe you were right and time would help. Especially after our last conversation."

"You said there was an issue with the hospital board?"

"Kelsey, please. Just hear me out. I swear I think it was all a set up. I made a mistake. A huge mistake I wish I could--"

"You *can't*. And this isn't the time for... Neil, it's over. If you brought me here to discuss the past, I'm leaving. I don't want to be too far away from JT in case he needs me." She lifted her chin and forced her gaze to meet his.

Thanks to her few previous boyfriends and lastly Neil, she'd learned a few lessons when it came to love. Like how life would bring you to your knees just to see if you would get up again.

"Fine. You're right. This isn't the place for this conversation but I hope now that we've seen each other again… I'm not going to stop trying, Kelsey. I want another chance. I hope one day you'll let me set the record straight and show you how much I regret what happened."

"Neil."

"Okay. Okay, Not now, but we owe each other that conversation, don't we? Now that time has passed?"

Closure. She wouldn't mind closure at all but getting it meant opening up fresh wounds. Could she do it? Was it worth it? In the end, what would it change? "Tell me what the Board said about JT."

Neil looked perturbed with her lack of agreement and notably uncomfortable with whatever he was about to say. She realized what that meant for a man normally so confident in his abilities and himself.

"You're not going to like it."

Chapter 5

Kelsey knew she wouldn't but there was no better time than the present. "Well, I'll never know unless you tell me, will I?"

"I've been asked—*told*—to hold JT for a mandatory psych evaluation."

She blinked, a knot instantly forming in the pit of her stomach. "*What*? Why? You can't be serious! They can't do that. Can they?"

"You're asking why after that write-up in the papers and what happened tonight? Kelsey...." Neil stared at her like she was as crazy as he apparently thought JT had become. "Your billionaire grandfather is dressing up as a homeless man and venturing out on the streets of New York City. At night. Alone. It's not normal behavior."

"But--"

"Sweetheart, JT sits on the hospital board. And not just this one but *multiple* boards and committees throughout the city. You can't be that surprised by their concern. They've seen the article, and there's a meme trending on social media about JT."

"What?"

"None of this looks good to anyone having any involvement with JT."

A meme? Seriously? Didn't people have better things to do than to make fun of an old man? "This can't be happening."

"It is," Neil murmured. "And it will look even worse if it appears as though the hospital isn't giving JT the care he obviously needs."

Oh, this was bad. Really, really bad. Because, like it or not, Neil made a good point. "I'll admit it's all very unorthodox but he has a right to *do* what he likes, to *go* where he likes, regardless of who he is or how old he is."

"Look, I hope JT's behavior isn't a sign of something bigger, *but* until we know for sure, you need to prepare yourself. The EMTs said when they arrived on the scene that JT tried to keep them away and was going on and on about taking that Devon guy home."

"Home? I don't understand. I thought JT was mugged in an alley."

"He was. JT said the 'Lowlanders' would care for Devon and JT tried to take him home by dragging Devon toward the underground."

Lowlanders? Where had she heard that term before? She rubbed her temple, and tried to recall. She was so tired.

"Kelsey, the police checked JT's cell phone and he didn't call for help. A delivery driver caught a glimpse of things and heard the gunshot. He's the one who called 911. Otherwise, who knows what might have happened or if JT would've gotten the man help at all."

"Oh, for the love of-- He would have. You *know* he would have. Neil, JT must have been in shock."

Oh, she didn't like Neil's expression. This wasn't good.

"Kelsey, JT tried to lift an injured man into some sort of vent or grate or something at the end of an alley. Do you have an explanation for that?"

"I—No, of course not, but I'm sure JT does." He would have one, right? JT wasn't… He wasn't….

Crazy?

"That may be so, but your grandfather's words and actions warrant a full medical and psychological evaluation. As his granddaughter, I would think you'd agree."

Rationally, she did. None of what Neil said about JT's behaviors made *any* sense. Why would JT do such a thing? But they weren't discussing a stranger. This was JT. And he wasn't crazy. "I understand keeping him for observation and running tests, but to admit him to the psych ward? *No.* I live with JT and he hasn't acted out of sorts around me. If anything, lately he seems sharper than ever, more focused and...driven."

It was true. For the last few months JT had displayed more energy and purpose, like his more active business days when he sought to close a deal and didn't stop until he'd achieved his goal.

"Then how do you explain his behavior? Better yet, tell me how to explain it to the board. Because unless you can, they have reason for concern."

And as such Neil had reason to back them instead of supporting JT? She shoved her hair off of her face and wished she had a vat of coffee. Something that would give her focus and energy and clarity. "Well, I'm no doctor but he was injured. He had to be scared and in pain. Pain and panic cause confusion, am I right? Especially in the elderly. Isn't that enough of an explanation? At least to justify *observation* in a regular hospital bed in lieu of a psych confinement?"

Neil frowned, as though pondering the legitimacy of her explanation. She could almost see the wheels in his brain turning, weighing her words and the leverage they'd hold. "Neil, please, let JT calm down, get some rest and the pain under control, and *then* talk with him. Don't make this decision just because the board is worried about public perception and pressuring you. You know your value here. They won't risk losing you."

"You want me to go to bat for JT."

"Why wouldn't you? You're a doctor who should put JT's well-being before all else. Not to mention the fact JT could've used his position on the board to have you replaced when... well, you know. But he *didn't*. He never once mentioned it, much less considered it, for all I know."

"They're not going to back down."

No, they wouldn't. But right now the important thing was buying some time to sort things out. "I know. I realize that. And maybe this means JT will need to step down from the board at a later date. Neil, he's not crazy. But, if the press were to find out you'd even considered such a thing they would have a field day. You know how they are. That kind of social stigma would negatively impact even the strongest of men, and despite privacy laws you know word would get out. Would you want that kind of publicity for your father or grandfather? Please, just stall the board for now and give JT some time to rest."

Neil remained silent a long moment and she sensed she was getting through to him.

"Do you know how long he's been going out there?"

She inhaled, hating to have to admit that she wasn't sure how long any of it had been happening.

And Lowlanders...

The word finally clicked in her brain and she struggled to not show any reaction on her features.

The Lowlanders?

Her love of books and stories began at a very young age when she would leave her parents' missionary and visit her grandparents before Christmas when her parents would arrive for the holidays. JT and Gram would take her all over the city to museums and galleries, theaters, and parks. Then at night JT would tell her stories of the city beneath New York City that was really a super secret workshop for--

Oh, boy.

It had to be the shock.

The fright of being mugged, injured.

Adrenaline. Nothing else.

Something about being out there and hurt had JT remembering the story as though it was real, and not a Christmas story he'd made up to entertain her when she visited. "No. No, I don't."

"Kelsey, I'm sorry. I can see how hard all of this is for you. I know you hate me for what I did to us. I hate me, too… but I still care for you. I still love you and I'm here for you. For whatever this turns out to be."

Snatched out of her thoughts, she blinked up at Neil. Torn between fear of what might be happening with JT, and the overwhelming desire to seek comfort in the arms of the man she'd loved so deeply. "If that's true then help me protect him." The words came out in a whisper that revealed too much. Bared too much. Made her vulnerable to a man who seemingly wanted to redeem himself. "Protect JT. Let me talk to him and get his version of things before you bow to the board and do something as drastic as a forced psychological evaluation. Okay?"

Neil leaned closer, gently grasped her arm and tugged her closer still. She placed her palms on his chest to keep from falling against him and she felt his lips brush the top of her head.

She closed her eyes, inhaled, and wished she could go back to how she'd felt before Neil's antics had been exposed. Back to when she'd trusted him and thought that maybe—just maybe—she'd found something real.

"Kelsey, I wish I could make this go away but a man got hurt tonight saving JT. They could've both been killed. If I ignore this and JT does something to endanger you…? I wouldn't be able to live with myself."

"JT would *never* let anything happen to me. You know that."

"He wouldn't *mean* for anything to happen. Just like he didn't mean for that Devon guy to get hurt tonight. But he did. And so could you."

She used her arms to push herself away from him, establishing some much needed distance. "I know. Okay? I know. But you wouldn't be responsible. I feel horrible about the other man's injury, but I know--*I know that I know*--there is a perfectly logical explanation for JT's behavior. Just give him time to rest and for me to talk to him. That's all I'm asking. Surely you can do that?"

Neil's gaze visibly softened and reminded her of

better days. She knew in that moment she'd won the argument--for the time being anyway.

"And in exchange... we can have that discussion I want as well?"

"You're using JT's condition to get what you want?"

Neil had the grace to look embarrassed. "Sweetheart, I'm desperate. And I'm asking you to hear me out, just like you're asking me to stall the board's request. I just want to talk."

He was right. She'd asked for time and so did he. It was only fair and she knew it. "Fine."

"Yeah?"

Neil smiled and she wasn't immune. Devastatingly handsome went a long way to describe him. The knee-weakening, heart-racing, kiss-me-now kind of handsome that went beyond lust to that of fairy tales and daydreams and happily-ever-afters. "We can talk--once JT is back home and settled in, and things have calmed down. But not until then." Hopefully she'd bought herself a little time, too. Time to evaluate her emotions for Neil now that some time had passed since their breakup.

"Okay. I can accept that. I'll happily accept that."

Neil pulled her into a hug, pressed a lingering kiss on her lips and released her.

"You won't regret it. It'll take some time to perform all the tests I want to do, but I can probably buy JT twenty-four hours to get his head together before the board demands follow-through on the psych evaluation. I'll do what I can but if JT's still confused... my hands are tied."

"I know. I understand." If JT was still confused in 24

hours there really was an issue to be addressed and she knew it couldn't be avoided.

His pager went off and after a quick glance Neil frowned and immediately began backing away at a brisk pace. "Thank you for the second chance. I won't screw it up."

"Neil, I said we'd *talk*, not--"

"I'll be back to check in on you both when I can. Gotta go!"

Neil grinned at her as he broke into a run, turning the corner before she could gather her scattered senses.

She stretched to ease the tension in her shoulders and wished it would get rid of the weight she felt pressing her toward the ground. She'd deal with Neil and set him straight about the difference between *talking* and *second chances* when the opportunity presented itself. Until then...

Would twenty-four hours be *enough*?

Chapter 6

Kelsey used the walk back to the ER to take some slow deep breaths and attempt to clear her mind of Neil's deliberate mistake. He knew what she'd said, he just wasn't going to give her a chance to clarify because she'd given him an in back into her life whether she liked it or not.

She turned the corner where she'd last glimpsed Neil and found activity outside of JT's cubicle. The staff were in the process of moving JT so she hurried toward them. "What's going on?"

"We've got his room ready," one of the orderlies said. "He'll have more privacy while he waits for the MRI."

JT's clothing had been placed in a bag at the foot of his bed along with the coat she'd left behind so Kelsey followed the orderlies pushing JT's bed past the many other people waiting in the Emergency Room, self-conscious because of the unfairness of it. JT had money and money bought a lot of things, like first class treatment in a hospital relying on his financial support for everything from research grants and new equipment to new hospital wings.

But what about the other people? What about-- "Wait, where's the other man? The one who was injured saving my grandfather?"

"I think he's still back in admitting," one of the attendants said with a tilt of his head.

Kelsey glanced at the hospital clerk accompanying them, the woman from earlier at the desk who'd shown her to JT's cubicle and flirted with Neil, and she nodded.

"I'm afraid so. He had no identification on him and no insurance information so they're waiting for him to wake up to sort things out."

"My grandfather will be paying the man's expenses. There's no need to worry about insurance now. He just needs a room and care as quickly as possible. I was on my way to see you about that but was delayed."

JT grasped her fingers in his and held tight, and a quick glance at his expression told her JT was gaining more awareness of the situation, and no doubt knew the delay was her going to battle with Neil on JT's behalf.

"Thank you, my dear. I'm so happy I have you."

"Always," she whispered. Whatever happened, whatever was said or done or implied, she would always have her grandfather's back just like he had always protected her. That's what family meant.

"Sweetheart, stay with Devon and make sure they do as I've asked. Please. I'll be fine and treated like a king, but I'll not rest easy unless I know Devon is being given the same care."

"Do you know him, Mr. Wallingford? You said his name is Devon? Do you know his last name?" the woman asked.

JT faltered for a moment. "It's not coming to me. But, yes, I know him, and he isn't to be billed a dime. Kelsey, see to it. He can share my room if there's not another one available."

"That isn't necessary, sir," the woman said.

"Sweetheart, stay with him and make sure it's done as I've asked."

"Ms. Jones," Kelsey said, reading the woman's nametag, "said she would take care of it. I want to go with you. JT, we need to talk about some things."

"I know. And we will. Later. I want you to stay with him while I rest. Don't let him out of your sight. I must know he's being taken care of properly."

Kelsey knew rest was best for him and talking now would only tire JT more, but she hated the thought of leaving him after the night's events. "Fine. I'll stay with him until he's settled in a room but then I'm coming to sit with you." There. A compromise with which even JT couldn't argue.

"That's my girl. Thank you, sweetheart."

She leaned low and pressed a kiss on his cheek then watched as the hospital staff wheeled JT onto an elevator to take him to his room.

"Oh, that patient is in 12C," the clerk called out to Kelsey just before the doors closed.

Once more Kelsey made her way back to the triage area of the Emergency Room, noting the cubicle numbers on the partitioned dividers as she walked by them.

12-C was on the left, the last unit on the end of the corridor toward the front.

She knocked softly and pushed back the curtain,

unsure of what she would find on the other side. A man, sure, but--

Definitely *not* the man lying so still in the hospital bed, a bandage on his forehead marked with a tinge of blood, and a bruise purpling his temple, eye, and upper cheek.

He looked to be in his early thirties. Tall, since his feet touched the footboard of the bed and his head and shoulders topped it. And good-looking, in a rough, roguish way, opposite of Neil's more classical handsomeness.

Roguish? You've been reading too many books from the romance section again.

But it was true. Even bruised and bandaged--or maybe because of it-- "Devon" was a man who drew one's attention with his close-cropped dark hair, whisker-scruff, and his broad shoulders filling the width of the bed to capacity. Dried blood remained on his face and bare chest and she realized JT's statement about Devon's wound bleeding had to have been an understatement.

"I see you've met sleeping beauty," a female voice said from behind Kelsey.

She turned and managed a weak smile at the nurse who'd entered the room. "Not officially. My grandfather—"

"I heard," the nurse said with a nod. "I just got the call and I've been assigned to personally take care of our patient until further notice. We'll get him moved upstairs as soon as an orderly is available. They're prepping a room now."

Once again JT's influence and finances were in action, and Kelsey was grateful for them, especially in moments like this. "Was he badly injured?"

"I'm sorry, but I'm not supposed to discuss his medical information with non-family."

"Oh...I see. Of course."

"But," the woman continued, lowering her voice so that only Kelsey could hear, "under the circumstances I can say that considering a bullet took some skin off of the side of his head, it could've been much worse. Head injuries always bleed a lot. Right now the docs just want to make sure they haven't missed something because he hasn't regained consciousness."

Her stomach clenched at the news. "Is he in danger? A coma?"

"No, no. He's unconscious, but not in a coma. As with any injury, there is always a risk, but more than anything his body has been through a trauma and sometimes they shut down on us to keep us from doing things we shouldn't. Given his size and obvious good shape," the nurse said with a smile, "my guess is that once he's awake he's going to be a hard man to keep still. The ones who look like him usually are."

Kelsey allowed her gaze to slide over his face and shoulders once more, a twinge of guilt nagging at her since she practically ogled the man. A carefully draped sheet left his chest bare, but even at rest she saw the delineation of his muscles. Whoever he was, he stayed in shape. "My grandfather wanted me to stay with him until he's settled. Is that all right?"

"No problem at all. Whatever Mr. Wallingford wants he gets. Make yourself comfortable. You can help protect him from all the nurses wanting to take a gander at him. Word spreads fast when we get one who looks like this."

Kelsey smiled at the woman's comment, well able to

understand why when her first thought upon seeing the man had been *roguish*. "Thanks. I'll let you know if he wakes up."

But what would happen then? Would Devon blame JT for his injury? Immediately call an attorney? The press?

One worry at a time. And right now that worry is Devon simply waking up.

The nurse checked the heart monitor and IV line and made some notes in his chart. Kelsey watched as only a bystander could, feeling helpless on the man's behalf.

"Okay, that's it for now. If he wakes up or you need anything, my name is Carla. Just press the red Call button on the bed and I'll be right in. Otherwise, I'm outside at the nurse's station."

"Thank you," Kelsey said, moving toward the cushioned, straight-backed chair beside the bed.

Carla left the room as quietly as she'd entered and Kelsey found herself alone with JT's rescuer. JT had called the man a friend, but who was he? Someone from Wall Street? A businessman working on a deal of some sort with JT?

She shook her head and frowned. Appearances were often deceiving but Devon definitely didn't look the type to be stuck in a three-piece suit.

So... a homeless man?

She found herself shaking her head once more, doubtful, but Devon *did* fit the profile of a former military man with his clean-cut looks and muscular build. So many soldiers fell through the cracks when they left the military, and JT donated to several charities that helped veterans in need.

When she was younger, she'd asked JT why he gave so much to veteran charities and he'd said it was to make up for his lack of service to his country. He'd told her how he'd escaped the draft for Vietnam due to already being married to Gram before the law had been changed drafting all men his age. The donations were his way of giving back and supporting all who'd served where he hadn't.

Maybe that was how JT knew Devon? Through one of the charities?

Kelsey glanced around the room until she spotted a clear plastic bag with the hospital's logo on the outside and dark material on the inside. She glanced at the curtain, feeling sneaky but determined. She wasn't stealing anything, after all. She just wanted answers. And to help the man who couldn't help himself at the moment.

She put her purse and coat in the uncomfortable-looking chair, went round the bed and opened the bag to take a look. She lifted the bag to her nose and took a cautious sniff, then inhaled deeper when Devon's cologne teased her senses. Whatever it was smelled woodsy and appealing. Whoever he was he definitely didn't *smell* like a homeless man. No, he smelled like spice and snow and pine. Her favorite scents, especially at this time of year.

He also had a penchant for black. Everything from his cold-weather blocking long-sleeve shirt to his slacks and sturdy leather boots were black in color, and all appeared to be relatively new.

She let her fingertips drift over the texture of his shirt, feeling the quality of the material. Did he have a coat?

Kelsey closed the pull-string bag and peeked into the tiny closet near the chair but didn't see anything. No coat. Seeing as how it was well below freezing outside he'd had to have worn one.

Ruined by all of the blood? Probably so. She made a mental list to replace the item before his release from the hospital, knowing JT would want that detail handled. Easy enough to do when a phone call and JT's name would have something delivered immediately.

Kelsey retraced her steps across the floor and sat on the edge of the bed by the man's long legs, drawn to him because he'd saved her grandfather's life.

What kind of man was he? Obviously one who ran toward danger instead of away from it seeing as how he'd saved an old man from what could have been his death. Maybe it was the bookstore owner inside of her who loved stories of all kinds, but it was all too easy to make up possible scenarios where Devon played the hero.

Her eyes burned with fatigue and she ached to find an empty bed. But sleep? Gritty eyes aside, she had enough adrenaline coursing through her veins from the fright of JT's ordeal to keep her awake for the next week.

Kelsey inhaled and stood, stretched once more and moved to the chair that gave her an unfettered look at JT's hero.

Sleeping Beauty... Who are you?

Chapter 7

"Kelsey? Sweetheart, wake up. *Kelsey?*"

Kelsey opened a bleary eye, totally lost as to where she was for a moment. It all came back in a rush and she jerked upright on the hospital cot, regretting her impulsive move when her head swirled like a merry-go-round.

"Kelsey?" JT said again.

She pulled the blanket the hospital had provided around her shoulders and shoved herself upright with one hand.

Nurse Carla had returned to Devon's bedside around 3 AM along with another woman and two men and they quickly and quietly set about moving Devon upstairs. She'd gathered her things and followed them back down the corridor to the elevator bank used to transport JT. They'd given Devon the room next to JT's to make it easier on her, with a cot in both rooms for her use if needed.

"My dear, are you awake?"

She nodded, eyes closed. "What's wrong? Are you all right?"

"I'm fine."

"Oh." Her confusion as to his urgency must have shown on her face because when she managed to force her eyelids up, JT waved her over to his side.

"Come, sit by me. We need to talk. *Kelsey*."

Wishing coffee would magically appear in front of her, she rubbed the grit from her eyes with the hem of the blanket.

"You always were a sleepyhead," JT murmured, his tone amused. "But I suppose you're due under the circumstances. Were you able to rest at all?"

She nodded, fully aware of the fact she was still half asleep and as groggy as JT guessed. "What time is it? Never mind. Doesn't matter. I'm coming," she said, stumbling to her feet and trying unsuccessfully to stifle a yawn. "I'm awake. See?" She shuffled over to his hospital bed dragging the hospital blanket with her for warmth, and sat down beside of him.

More than anything she wanted to snuggle up by his side, lay her head on his shoulder and sleep like she had as an orphaned child, safe in his arms. The entire year after her parents' death she'd had nightmares and often wound up in the living room recliner snuggled on JT's lap. Not once had he ever complained, regardless of whether he had an important business meeting the following morning.

She shook her head and rubbed her eyes again, stifling a yawn. "You should be resting. Are you feeling all right?"

"Yes, yes. I'm much better today."

She released the ends of the blanket to take his

thick, wrinkled hand in hers and smoothed her fingers over the top. He did look better. Exhausted, but better. "Good. Maybe now that we've both gotten a few hours of sleep, you can explain what's going on and what happened last night?"

"Yes, I plan to, but first-- Kelsey... I'm sorry for waking you but there's no time to spare."

"Something *is* wrong." Oh, why couldn't she be a morning person who woke up ready to tackle the world with a blaze of energy? It took time for her to clear the cobwebs and get enough caffeine into her system for her to greet the day with anything more than a mumbled "good morning" she didn't really feel.

"Yes, I'm afraid it is," JT said. "The nurse came in while you were sleeping."

"She did?" She'd slept through that? "What's wrong? Did she say something about your test results?"

"No, no. Not about me, my dear. It's Devon."

"What about him? Is he awake? He didn't *die*, did he?" That thought flooded her body with much needed adrenaline-fueled clarity, but thankfully JT shook his head.

"He's awake--but he doesn't remember. Not anything. Amnesia, the nurse said. Caused by the bullet grazing his head."

Amnesia? Didn't that only happen in books? "Oh. That's... terrifying."

"It is. I can't imagine what he's going through right now. But, Kelsey, I need to tell you something. That's why I woke you. Devon isn't who he seems."

"He's not?"

"No. At least I don't think so. My dear, you must

have an open mind and hear me out before you rush to conclusions."

She blinked and wondered if this was going to be a Lowlander story like those Neil described because if so she *really* needed caffeine to prep for it. "O-kay," she murmured, bracing herself for whatever was about to come next.

"Kelsey, do you remember the bedtime stories I told you years ago?"

No, no, no! Any and all remnants of fog cleared completely, driven away by JT's question. "You told me lots of stories, Poppy. What about them?" *Please don't say it. Don't let Neil be right.*

"Kelsey, he's one of them. Devon is a *Lowlander*."

Air left her lungs in a silent whoosh and she sat there, unable to breathe. Something had happened to JT. Something big. Maybe a stroke? "You think he's a... Lowlander? From the bedtime story?"

"Yes. I believe he is. I'm nearly certain of it, but never could get a concrete answer from Devon about who he works for. Then again I'd have been surprised if he'd actually said. Security is so important."

"Security...?"

"Kelsey, the tales I told you as a child--they weren't just make believe. *I* was the little boy who was raised in Yorkton. The one who left to make his fortune, although, truth be told, there was more to it than that."

Kelsey stared at her grandfather, at a loss, heart breaking because of what his words meant and how they would impact the future. *Oh, Poppy.*

She wasn't ready for this. Wasn't ready to lose him. Maybe she wasn't losing him in the physical sense, but mentally....

"That's why I've been dressing up, Kelsey. I've been searching for the way home. To Yorkton. I must get home one last time. Before it's too late."

She really wished someone would jump out from within the bathroom to say she was being pranked. Because the longer she sat there, the more time there was for his words to sink in, and the more she realized nothing would ever be the same. The world as she knew it was officially changing. Again. And like last time it came with the price of loss. "You've been doing all of this because... You think the stories are real."

"I don't think it, my girl. I know it. Yorkton must remain hidden, guarded, which is why I haven't been able to find my way back yet, but Devon is the key."

JT nodded as though the movement would confirm his words, his gaze lit with a gleam she hadn't seen in him in a very long time. Was this why he'd seemed more focused of late? Because of... *this*?

But that meant whatever had happened to make him believe the stories were real had happened what? Months ago? How could she not have noticed the change? "And Devon is the key because you think he's...."

"My way home," he said with a commanding nod. "Sweetheart, there's so much to tell you. So much we must do. But Devon... We'll have to be very careful with him so that when his memory retu-- You don't believe me."

———————————

Chapter 8

———————————

Kelsey struggled to keep her expression from revealing more than it should. Fought to hide her fear and outright panic because her strong, healthy, wonderful grandfather was now acting like a child, his mind full of fantasy and outrageous plans. "It's a little hard to wrap my head around the idea, that's all."

Silence followed her words and JT's gaze lost a bit of its gleam.

"I suppose it is." Disappointment laced his voice. "I've been a fool. I was so excited I simply assumed you would believe me, but I see now that's not the case."

He seemed so hurt by the fact she hadn't immediately jumped up and down with excitement at his announcement, but-- How could she? "JT, it's been a very long night and neither one of us has had much rest. Maybe--"

"Oh, don't give me that, Kelsey Anne. I know what I'm saying. I may be old but I'm in complete possession of my senses. Now I ask you to have an open mind and hear me out."

Kelsey blinked away the hot sting of tears and looked down at their hands layered atop one another, her heart breaking into a million pieces bit by painful bit.

JT wouldn't handle being confined in a hospital ward well. Being poked and prodded and questioned by doctors. Medicated. He was a man who prided himself on his intellect in making solid, multi-million dollar business deals that had grown over time. How could he possibly *believe*... "Of course. I'm listening." The words emerged thick and choked and she cleared her throat and tried again. "Tell me. I'm listening."

"Oh, my dear. There's no need for tears."

No need? She shook her head and managed a weak laugh. "Poppy, they were just *stories*. An underground city? *Under* New York City? It isn't possible."

"You said you'd listen."

She squeezed her eyes tight and clasped his hand tighter. "I *promise you* I will listen to every word, but if Neil comes in and you tell him what you just told me..."

"Kelsey, I am *not* confused. I'll admit to being shaken up after the mugging or else I wouldn't have said a word to those dunderheads about Devon, but I'm thinking clearly now. And those stories I told you as a child were fact. *I* left Yorkton when I was nineteen years old. *I'm* the boy who grew up in Yorkton after my parents, along with the Klaas family and everyone involved in our mission, were driven underground during the mob wars of the 1930's. It was safer there, away from the violence, and they were able to continue on."

"Working for... Santa?" It was the first time she'd

referenced that part of the story and she held her breath, waiting for his response.

"Yes."

"Okay," she said, unsure of what else to do except play along. "For the sake of-- Let's say it's all true." She ignored his disgruntled expression and kept going. "If you left this Yorkton place then *why* do you want to go back? How are you sure it's even still there? And why can't you find them without dressing up and endangering yourself?"

He grimaced, his lined features showing every moment of his advancing years. "I couldn't very well go into the tunnels dressed in my Armani suits, now could I? But that's neither here nor there. What's important right now is Devon's care. The doctors say the amnesia is temporary and his memory will return in a few days, maybe a week. Other than his memory loss, however, he's fine and the nurse says they could release him as early as tomorrow."

"So soon?" Didn't getting a gunshot--graze--constitute a longer stay? It's not like the hospital had to worry about his medical bills going unpaid.

"Apparently now that he's awake, he's a handful and he thinks leaving may help him remember."

"Oh." She hadn't thought of it from that perspective. "Well, I'm sure his family has arrived by now and will help him while he recovers."

"Kelsey..." JT shifted his hand to squeeze her fingers. "No one has claimed Devon, nor will they claim him. It's against the rules. He shouldn't have left the tunnels to help me. But now that he has, it's up to us to take care of him. That's why I woke you. We must make arrangements for when he's released."

JT looked exhausted. Deep shadows stained the skin beneath his eyes and his face had a puffiness to it and gray-toned color she didn't remember seeing before. "What kind of arrangements?"

This was the JT she knew and loved. Caring, kind, thoughtful. Someone who looked out for others, no matter the cost.

She leaned forward and JT lifted his hand to her cheek, the pad of his thumb brushing lightly back and forth across her skin. His gaze was direct, clear. And had she not just listened to him talk of secret cities and tunnels and *Santa*, she would've thought him perfectly fine.

"Kelsey, you know my health isn't the best. The medication I take can only do so much and eventually my heart will give out. When that happens... I want to have peace with those I left behind. And I want to be home."

Oh, how she hated it when he talked this way. "Poppy, arrangements can be made. I'll make sure you're home and comfortable. We can hire doctors and nurses to come to the penthouse. It'll be okay."

Tears blurred her eyes but she refused to let them fall. Now wasn't the time. She had to be strong. For his sake. And hers.

"Kelsey, that penthouse was my way of coming out on top when I had started lower than low, *below* ground. To be honest, part of the reason for my success was the anger I had driving me."

She struggled to follow the change in conversation. "Anger from what?"

JT lowered his gaze and his expression changed, saddened. Took on a distant look filled with mixed emotions she couldn't decipher. "A broken heart. I fell in love, deeply in love, with a woman who chose another."

That hadn't been part of the story he'd told her as a child. Only that the young man had found love and had a family. A granddaughter who lived in a far away land... "But I thought Gram...?"

A sweet smile formed on his lips.

"Your grandmother healed me. Helped me. And I'll love her forever. But she wasn't my first love."

"I'm sorry."

Kelsey watched as his gaze sharpened once more, like he shoved the memories into a compartment to return to the here and now.

"As am I. That's why I need to return and... apologize for things I said before I left. I have wrongs to make right before I go to my Maker, Kelsey, and this--Devon, and the truth I know which you believe is only a story--is part of it."

She had to tread carefully. Softly. But it was crazy! All of it crazy.

But he was *her* crazy and she loved him more than anything. He was her person. The one—the only—person she had to call her own.

Why was this happening? It wasn't fair. He was all she had left in this world. Why him?

JT believed every word he spoke. She could see it in his eyes. Hear it in his voice. Feel it in the intensity surging out of him.

She didn't believe a word of it. How could she? An underground city no one knew about?

Santa's workshop?

It was ridiculous.

But more importantly, how was she going to protect

JT from himself? From the hospital board, the press? All of those who would happily take advantage of this weakness? Exploit JT out of pure greed?

"I'll explain more to you when there's time, but until you know the whole story, please, just do as I ask, Kelsey. You have to trust me and believe and not allow your mind to disregard something because it isn't considered possible. *All things* are possible. You should know that."

She inhaled and quickly decided that now wasn't the time to sugarcoat anything. "Neil says the hospital board thinks you need a *mandatory* psych evaluation. JT, I begged Neil for more time last night because of your injuries but if they heard you now, saying these things...."

She'd hurt him yet again with her words. She could see it in his expression and her stomach clenched because of it. The last thing she'd ever do is deliberately hurt him but how could he believe something like-- *that?*

"I don't care what any of those fools think. The only person I need to believe me is you."

"Don't you see? It doesn't matter whether I believe you or not. That's not the priority. Poppy, they want to *commit* you because of your behavior. The hospital board is pressuring Neil and you *know* how much power they have. Power they will use *against* you. You have to stop saying these things. You're going to wind up in an institution and there won't be anything I can do."

"My dear, I haven't lost my mind. If anything, I've finally remembered what's important. All my life I've worked and, yes, I found love again with your grandmother, but ever since she died and my health has declined, my worry is for you. I had--have--family in Yorkton. Brothers, a sister, all of whom would have had children, grandchildren--your family. Maybe I don't know who is still alive or dead, but I want to know. It's burdened me my entire life and before I die..." His voice broke and tears sparkled in his eyes. "Kelsey, I don't even know how my parents passed. If they were sick or if they went peacefully in their sleep. I *need* to know these things."

She bit her lip and fought back tears, unable to stand the sight of JT crying, unable to bear the pain in his words. But the reality? "JT, you're an only child."

"For heaven's sake, Kelsey Anne. What else could I say when asked about my family? When you leave the Lowlands, you leave everything and everyone behind for their protection. I left in 1960, during the Cold War, when it was dangerous to hold secrets of any kind. But I was desperate to get away. I couldn't bear seeing the woman I loved with another man."

So maybe this crazy story was one of protection? His brain's muddled way of handling that devastation and betrayal? Combine those with possibly a stroke or clot or whatever event he'd suffered and that made it real to him?

"My dear, before you start agreeing with the others condemning me simply because I'm getting old, please, give me time to tell the whole story, not just the child's version you know. Then, you'll understand and hopefully —eventually—I can show you Yorkton, with Devon's help."

Show her?

Chapter 9

"Who is this Devon person? How did you meet?"

"We met there," he said simply. "In the tunnels. He's one of them. Though, like I said, he hasn't outright confirmed it."

"He's a Lowlander?"

"Yes."

"And when you say you met in the tunnels you mean you went down there, actually traveled back into the subway tunnels? *Alone?*"

Numb. With every question she asked, and every answer he gave, she grew more and more numb. Out of fear, desperation. Horror. Whatever it was that made it clear her reality—her life with JT—changed with his reply. She was going to lose JT to this madness, if she hadn't already.

She knew better than to think he meant the subway stations populated by NYC's finest but the darker, more sinister areas off-limits to the public, home to those brazen enough--tough enough--to enter. When she thought of the horrible things that could have happened to him and what *had* happened...

"How else am I supposed to reconnect with my family?"

"JT, I'm your family. *Me*. Why would you do such a thing?"

"I'm doing this *for* you, my dear. And for myself. Going into the tunnels was risky, yes, but I am well aware of the danger." He released a frustrated sound. "Kelsey, you're focusing on things that do not matter and not on those that do."

"By all means, let's not focus on your health and the extreme danger you put yourself in but on *Santa's workshop*." The words spilled out in her exhausted anger and she hurried to clamp a hand over her lips. It was too late though. They hung there in the air between them, in all their ugliness and crazy.

"I'm here now, aren't I? I'm fine."

This was a long, *long* way from fine. "If you've been going below, how did they find you in an alley?"

"There are many ways to enter and exit the underground. It's traversing the tunnels that's difficult."

"I'm sure they are." She stared at JT. At the bruises so dark on his face, the puffiness of his mouth, and the cut on his lip. How could she get through to him? Make him understand?

"Kelsey, I didn't plan on telling you. Not yet. Not until I'd made contact and was assured the Elder Council would allow us to return."

"*Us*?" Oh, her head was really starting to pound. Now he was trying to suck her into his fictional underground city? Drag her into a grate in a dark alley like he had with Devon?

"Of course, us. I want you to see it, my dear. For you to know where you're from and meet your family so you won't be alone when I'm gone. It's taken me longer than I thought it would to find an entry point to the inner tunnels. Once you're down there it's very confusing, and then you run into men like Devon who lead you away from Yorkton. There are many safeguards in place to protect it. One simply can't go there, even if I could find my way through the maze below ground."

Her mind whirled with all he'd said, his story versus... reality. "So all of this is because you've been trying to find Yorkton."

"Yes."

Bad enough to go out on the streets and alleys as he obviously had, but God only knew what could have happened below ground. He could have run into bad people who would've hurt him, or simply tripped and fallen, broken a bone or hit his head, died down there, and never been found! She would've never known what happened to him... "JT, can't you see what you're doing is-- It sounds...." She couldn't bring herself to say the word.

"Crazy? Most people would agree, Kelsey, but you're thinking from your mind, not from your heart, and that's how you must think. Kelsey, you've refused to celebrate Christmas since your parents were killed, and when my dear Patricia died there simply didn't seem to be any point in fighting with you like she did to put up a tree and celebrate the day."

"What does *that* have to do with *this*?" It wasn't that she didn't celebrate Christmas but that she didn't celebrate the holiday as it had been made to be. Christmas was a time of mourning for her. Her parents had died two days before Christmas, her grandmother right afterward several years later. It felt wrong to decorate and exchange gifts. Disrespectful.

"Some people don't believe in the meaning of Christmas but it's real and meant to be rejoiced. It's just as real as Yorkton and all that it stands for."

Had he really just made that comparison? God and Santa? "Seriously?"

JT pursed his lips, a frown pulling his bushy eyebrows low.

"Kelsey Anne, I'm not going to take you to task for that tone or not believing me now, but I do expect an apology when you realize I'm telling the truth."

Oh, how her head pounded. Kelsey stared at her grandfather, torn between the urge to cry and the desire to take him by the shoulders and shake him, try to wake him from this fantasy he'd created.

Lowlanders. Santa's secret workshop. A needed move from the North Pole due to the popularity of a certain book read every Christmas Eve.

An entire city beneath New York City bustling with people and—bicycles.

JT had told her everyone walked or rode bicycles. There was a school, a church. Shops. Streetlights. A hidden world where the Christmas magic supposedly happened, all out of duty and honor. Service.

The bedtime story came back to her bit by bit. But as much as she loved books and stories, she didn't believe in romance heroes or fairytales, folklore or super-secret cities. They were just stories.

But doesn't every story contain at least a tiny bit of truth?

Coffee. She needed coffee and lots of it. She also needed time. Time to pray, think, and research in order to figure out the proper decisions regarding JT's care and the help he obviously needed. Time to reflect and come to terms with these changes, when all she wanted was to go back and be a little girl again where JT protected her and took care of everything, and make-believe stories were normal and fun.

Wait... Did something about this actually make sense? "Are you saying *that's* why the press has never been able to confirm your childhood?" It had been a source of contention for years. How could a man who'd risen through the ranks of the publishing industry and gone on to earn financial greatness simply appear out of nowhere? Eventually the story grew that JT was an orphan lost in the cracks of a burgeoning, problematic, and growing system, but was this true?

"Yes. Kelsey, I'll answer any questions you have but only on the condition that you do not share what I tell you with Neil or anyone else. You have no idea the harm it would do for word to get out that Yorkton exists. People would flood the tunnels in search of it."

Not tell anyone? No one would believe her, anyway.

"The cause being the greater good."

"To put it simply, yes. You remember," he said, sounding pleased. "The Lowlanders are called to help others, to serve and help those in need, but they do many other things. Have done some world-changing things."

"Such as?"

JT frowned at her, his gaze wary. "Let's just say the world would be a much, much darker place if not for those willing to sacrifice and serve."

Chapter 10

She opened her mouth to ask another question but couldn't form the words. The truth came down to this: JT had always loved her, protected her, and he'd never lied to her. The bond they shared was one of trust and respect and love, and that was something she had to defend from Neil and the hospital board if nothing else. "This is a lot to grasp."

"I know. And if given the opportunity, I had planned to show you instead of trying to convince you like this, but you must give your word to protect the Lowlanders. It's imperative."

"Of course." That was a promise easy enough to keep. "I'll protect the secret." *And you.*

Emotions flooded her. Sadness and grief. A keen sense of loss. She didn't believe JT had suffered a psychotic break but her grandfather was obviously in the midst of some sort of medical issue. Why else would he be talking this way?

"Good. Now, this is what I want you to do. Go to Devon's room and introduce yourself, check on him. He must be frightened at not being able to remember, but tell him I know him, and that he's my friend. That everything is going to be fine. We'll take care of everything and he has nothing to worry about."

Kelsey closed her eyes and fought for patience. Neil would come check on JT sometime today and decide whether or not he was going to have to enforce the requested psych evaluation. Thanksgiving was only a few days away. Christmas was only a matter of weeks. She couldn't stand the thought of JT being held against his will. Which meant she had to get JT out of the hospital and find discreet, professional help. Maybe a specialist from a different hospital? A private clinic somewhere overseas?

How do you hide a well-known billionaire? Were there protocols for such things?

"Kelsey?"

"I'm listening." She nodded. She made eye contact. She did all the things she felt she was supposed to do while her mind continued to whirl.

"Once Devon's memory returns he will immediately go to ground. If I have any hope of finding Yorkton and appearing before the Elder Counsel, I have to convince Devon to help me. I need him and that means hanging onto him as long as possible. Please, my dear. Do this for me. Make it my Christmas wish, if you will. The last wish of a man who knows his time is limited."

Ohhh, kick her when she's down! JT *never* asked her for anything!

In all of the years he'd cared for her, he'd given her everything. A home, love, and stability. A career and bookstore unlike any in the city. Yes, she'd made her business a success, but it was because of him that it was hers. And it was all--*all*--done out of love for her.

"Give me this time until Devon's memory returns to convince him to help me. That's all I ask."

"You don't ask for much, do you?" she murmured, even though she knew in her heart she'd give him the world if she could. "JT, Neil will be here at any moment. How are you going to explain your actions to him? What happens if you tell Devon where you think he's from and *he* goes running to Neil or—or the press?"

"Kelsey... Give me the time I'm asking for and... I will stop dressing up and going underground as a home-less man. Otherwise, I will be forced to continue my search for a way home."

"That's blackmail."

"That's business," her grandfather countered, his gaze not only clear but shrewd. "And a very fair trade, if I say so myself. You don't want me in the tunnels and while you're questioning the truth of what I've said, you know very well that I haven't lost my mind. But, only time will tell. You need time to come to a decision about my mental capacity, just like I need this time with Devon. So, do we have a deal?"

"Extortion." She shook her head. "I'm your grand-daughter. I just want you to be safe and healthy and you're blackmailing me? Maybe you *should* talk to someone about...all of this?"

"I will talk to someone--Devon."

"He's not a therapist," she said, thoroughly exasper-ated. "I mean, is he? Is that how you know him?" Could that be the connection between the two men? Why Devon just happened to be there trying to help her grandfather last night?

JT chuckled. "If it makes you feel better to think of Devon as a therapist, then please do so, my dear. But he's actually security."

Security. All of the talk about the underground and the black clothes and the muscles and-- "Is he with *the mob*?"

JT chuckled and then coughed, wincing from the pain of his bruised ribs. "Oh, my girl. Your imagination is running rampant, isn't it? No, he is not. He introduced himself to me as security," he repeated. "And my every dealing with him has been in that capacity. I believe he is one of Yorkton's many guards. Now, what is your decision? Will you help me? Just until the boy's memory returns."

Best case scenario? When Devon's memory returns, he doesn't verify JT's story. JT would then realize Devon isn't a Lowlander and JT would see that he's not thinking clearly and seek help.

Worst case scenario?

You sooo don't want to go there.

Could she really refuse? Devon had saved her grandfather's life and by going along with JT in this crazy plan of his, she would at least be kept in the know. Otherwise her grandfather could take matters into his own hands-- again--and do who knew what.

It's just for a little while. A few days. Maybe a week.

If what JT said was true about the timetable for Devon's memory to return. And if someone showed up at the hospital claiming to know Devon, the staff and police would know who to contact and where Devon was recuperating. In the meantime, maybe JT would return to his senses--especially since Devon *didn't* confirm Yorkton's existence? Oh, it all made her head pound. "I don't like this."

"I know. But do you agree?"

"Fine."

"You agree? You'll let me have this time with Devon until his memory returns?"

She reluctantly nodded. "Agreed. I don't have much of a choice, do I? But for the record? Let me make it perfectly clear that this—*all of this*—is a really, really bad idea."

"But you'll call and make sure Rita prepares a room for him?"

"Wait, what? You asked for time with Devon. You mean you want to take him *home* with us?"

"Where else would he go?"

"A hotel? It's New York. There certainly isn't a lack of them. He's a stranger, JT."

"He's not a stranger."

"Isn't he? You said you *think* he's from this Yorkton place but…."

"He is. I'm sure of it."

"But what if he's not? You're not sure, you said as much earlier. You saw him in the tunnels, right? So what if he's just a guy? Someone working down there or conducting the sort of business that has to be done in the dark, below ground, because it's so *illegal*?"

"Bah, child. You act as if I haven't spent the majority of my life in New York with businessmen who were more dangerous than the people you speak of. Devon is one of them. I'm sure of it."

"JT, Devon would be perfectly fine at a hotel. If it makes you feel better we can find a suite near the penthouse where you can--"

"No, no, my girl. Devon is staying with us. I insist."

Chapter 11

Devon pretended to be asleep when the door to his room opened for what had to be the hundredth time since he'd woken and discovered he was in the hospital.

Those few hours earlier, a doctor had been called, greeting him and calling him Devon. The doc then gave him a physical before asking if he had any questions.

It was then that he'd realized he had a blank slate for a brain because he neither recognized his name, nor could he remember how he'd come to be there.

The next hour or so was spent going over his test results and answering--or rather *not* answering--questions. What was his last name? His address? Did he know how to tie his shoes? What color were his eyes? Who was the president? How tall was he? What year was it? Did he know the month? Was he married? Living with someone? Who was his emergency contact? Was he from New York?

The doc finally diagnosed him with temporary amnesia. His memory, the doctor stated, would return when his body healed from the shock and trauma of a bullet scraping the side of his head near his temple. Other than his lack of memory, he appeared to be in good health.

But now Devon listened closely, tracking this woman's movements as she crossed the room toward his bed. He could recognize that she was not a nurse or member of the staff. None of *them* moved that slowly or quietly.

He opened his eyes and heard her suck in a surprised gasp. No, this visitor definitely wasn't like the others.

Despite his aching head he took in her appearance, noting the lack of photo ID tag or scrubs. Blond hair fell over her shoulders in thick, wavy curls and even though she looked like she could use some sleep, he appreciated her beauty. He'd have to be blind not to.

Did she know him? Had she come to identify him? The man in him was intrigued, his interest piqued.

Was she his girlfriend?

You'd be mighty lucky if that's the case.

Or wife?

Even luckier. "Do I know you?"

"No. I'm sorry to disturb you."

"I wasn't asleep. Who are you?"

She held out her hand for him to shake.

"I'm Kelsey Richards. The man you helped last night is my grandfather. I can't thank you enough for what you did for him, but I am very sorry you were hurt in the process."

He grasped her small hand in his, liking that she had a firm grip despite the exhausted hollows shadowing her gray-green eyes. Devon stared into the depths of her gaze, struck by the unusual color combination. "Glad I could be of service."

Kelsey flashed a quick smile and looked a little uncomfortable as she retrieved her hand and shoved it into the pocket of her sweater. "Again, I just wanted to say thank you."

"He was mugged, right?"

Her full lips parted and her eyes widened.

"You remember what happened?"

He hated to squash the hope and excitement he saw in her expression. "No. The doctor told me this morning."

Her shoulders fell a bit as her disappointment weighed her down once more. "Oh. Of course. I'm sorry. I just thought... Well, you know."

Yeah, he did. Or rather--didn't. She wasn't the only one disappointed at his lack of memory. "What's your grandfather's name?" Somehow he knew these were the polite questions to ask under the circumstances, even though he found himself lost in the void of his mind.

"JT Wallingford."

Her gaze studied him closely, searching, waiting for recognition. "Right. The doc told me earlier but it didn't register. Still doesn't sound familiar, though. Can you tell me anything else? My last name would be a good start."

She smiled again, though this time it seemed more forced. "I'm sorry, no. I have no idea. You aren't one of his acquaintances I'm familiar with so I'll leave those questions for JT to answer. He'd like to talk to you as soon as you're up to it, and he also wanted me to tell you not to worry. He's taken care of your medical expenses."

He hadn't even thought of how he'd go about paying for the hospital stay. Did he have a job? Some sort of insurance? Whether he did or he didn't he felt bad at the thought of the old man footing the expense. "That's very generous of him, but not necessary."

"It's taken care of. He insists, so no worries there, okay? Your job is to simply heal and get your memory back. That's the most important thing."

"Uh... Okay." He lifted his hand and rubbed the back of his neck. "I'm not sure what to say. Please give him my thanks until I can see him to say it myself."

"I will." She sank back on her boot heels before shifting from foot to foot. "JT and I--everyone--hope your memory returns as quickly as possible but, um, JT also wanted me to tell you that if you're released before that happens, he's made arrangements for your lodging as well."

Devon stared at Kelsey Richards. The offer she outlined went above and beyond generous, but seeing as how the doc had said he hadn't had a wallet in his possession when he got to the hospital, Devon knew better than to argue. For the moment anyway. "Expenses and a place to stay?"

Hard to go home when you can't remember where you live.

He searched his empty memory bank for some thought of who JT Wallingford was and fought his frustration at not being able to place the man. He didn't regret aiding Kelsey's grandfather, but the wall of nothing where his memory used to be was getting tiresome already. "Word's getting around that I want to get out of here, huh?"

A throaty laugh softened her features and added to her appeal.

"No one likes staying in the hospital so it's perfectly

understandable. JT's anxious to leave as quickly as he can, too."

"Maybe the doc will release us soon then."

"Maybe," she said, taking a step back and eyeing the door like she wanted to bolt. "Okay, so, the doctors are running more tests on JT. After that I'm sure he will need some rest but if you're feeling up for a walk later this afternoon, I'm sure he'd welcome a visit. He's next door, on the left."

"I look forward to speaking with your grandfather." If he wanted to find out who he actually was, JT Wallingford was apparently the person with whom to start.

"Good. Try to get some rest. I'll see you later, when you come to visit JT. Nice to meet you, Devon."

"Likewise." Devon watched her leave his room, the sway of her hips and the length of her long hair drawing his attention.

He shut down his thoughts with a shake of his head. He was in the hospital with no memory of who he was or where he came from and yet he was noticing Kelsey Richards?

Not a good idea. He didn't even know if he was free to notice her. For all he knew he could have a wife and kids waiting for him at home.

But if that were the case, wouldn't someone have come searching for him by now?

Chapter 12

Devon stared at the closed door for quite a while before shifting in the uncomfortable bed, fatigue dragging at him despite the fact he'd only just woken up. He hated being stuck in bed. Hated the pounding in his head and the way a simple trip to the bathroom seemed to require Herculean effort.

Frustrated, he grabbed the TV remote off of the tray table beside the bed and pressed the ON button. The small screen across the room filled with color and he watched about twenty seconds of a commercial on identity theft before grumbling and flipping the channel. That was something else he probably needed to worry about, but since he didn't know if he'd been carrying a wallet before the mugging, it was hard to report whether or not it was stolen.

"The Carolinas and all of the eastern seaboard are bracing for a very late season hurricane and we might just see some of the rain from that system here in New York City later this week. Here's Sheila McMurphy with the full report."

Another channel change landed on a picture of an

old man dressed in a tuxedo paired with another picture of the same man dressed rather shabbily.

"There's a new development concerning billionaire JT Wallingford. Last night the seventy-eight year old businessman was taken to the hospital after an apparent mugging. A recent tabloid photo, shown on the left of your screen, depicted Mr. Wallingford dressed in rags as he wandered the streets. A hospital source who asked to remain anonymous stated Mr. Wallingford is resting comfortably with only minor injuries, however, the man who came to Wallingford's aid to fight off his captors sustained a gunshot wound. No word yet on that man's condition. Both are being treated while under protective custody due to the robbery attempt and Wallingford's recent behavior, which has been described as unusual. Our investigative reporter Muriel Benson has this to say."

The screen changed to that of a reporter standing outside of what looked to be a bookstore on a busy street.

"JT Wallingford is known for many things, mainly his wealth and business acumen since it's how he built his publishing empire during the 1980's. But recently the semi-retired Wallingford has had to make several trips to well-known hospitals and with the disclosure of the 'homeless photos', as many are calling them, some wonder if JT Wallingford's mental clarity is deteriorating. Mr. Wallingford's attorney issued a statement of 'No comment' and press agencies from around the globe were handed restraining orders demanding a minimum distance from Mr. Wallingford and his domain at all times. We will keep you posted with any new information on this strange story as we receive it."

The news continued but Devon lost interest, his mind focused on Kelsey's exhausted appearance and genuine gratitude. No wonder she was so thankful he'd been there to help her grandfather, especially if what the news reporter said was true about his health and mental state.

Devon lifted his hand to his head and lightly touched the bandage covering the gunshot wound, wincing at the pain.

Think.

How did he know JT Wallingford?

What was his last name?

Why hadn't someone come searching for him or at least ask about him via a description since he hadn't returned home last night?

He didn't like the responses his brain fired back at him, thoughts that maybe he had no family or significant other in his life *to* miss him. And if he didn't, what kind of man did that make him that no one cared?

He spotted a small closet opposite the bed and shoved back the covers. Maybe if he went through his clothing. Saw it. Felt it. Maybe it would trigger something?

Anything was better than stewing over all of the blanks where his memories should be.

Devon pulled the line of his IV to bring the mobile unit close enough to use as a crutch and forced himself to his feet, thankful someone had at least dressed him in hospital scrub pants.

Several steps away from the bed a wave of dizziness washed over him, leaving him shaking and holding on to the metal rod like a lifeline.

"What are you *doing*?"

Kelsey's voice sliced through his confusion and encroaching black spots dotting the space in front of his eyes. He felt her more than saw her approach and gripped her shoulder when she placed his IV-free arm around her while her other arm encircled his waist.

"Back to bed. Come on. This way."

He followed her urging, not wanting to do anything else to embarrass himself in front of her. Like falling face-first at her feet.

"Turn. Sit. Good."

"Sounds like you're talking to a dog."

"Sorry. Guess I'm used to talking to Bronte."

Bronte?

Something about the name tugged at him but disappeared before it could fully register. He focused and tried to retrieve whatever it was that had disappeared like a mist.

There was something about the name but what was it?

"She's our Labradoodle and can be a bit stubborn when she wants to be."

So she *was* talking to him like a dog.

What was it with women and dogs?

This time an image flashed through his head. There, then gone. Something to do with snow and dogs and-- *snowshoes?*

That didn't make sense. The snow might be deep in the city at times but he doubted snowshoes were ever a necessity.

"What were you doing up? Do you need to go to the restroom?"

If he did he certainly wouldn't tell her. Drawn from his thoughts he pointed toward the closet. "My clothes," he said. "I wanted to get them and see if they might help me remember."

"You are determined, aren't you? I would be, too."

"The doc says it's best if I remember on my own. I don't want to wait until I get the chance to talk to your grandfather to find out what he knows about me."

"I understand. Stay put. I'll get your clothes for you."

He didn't track her progress across the room but instead closed his eyes and willed the dizziness away. "Why did you come back?"

"What? Oh, I came back to ask if you liked steak or chicken? JT is already complaining about the hospital food, so I thought I would order something special for dinner while you two talked."

"I like both," he said, not understanding *how* he knew but simply knowing he did. "But I'm fine with the food here. Don't go to any trouble."

He opened his eyes just as she returned to stand before him, a plastic bag gripped in her hands.

"It's no trouble. Really. JT's very special to me. I don't know what I'd do without him."

Her voice held a hint of sadness and fear that drew his attention and reminded him of what he'd heard on the news. "Why do you say it like that? Is JT--your grandfather all right?"

Her lashes lowered, shielded her eyes. "Oh, it's… I'm worried about him. That's all."

Kelsey held out the plastic bag and their fingers brushed in the exchange. She had such soft, small hands. Delicate but strong. "Thanks."

"You're welcome. Devon? You're going to be okay. Neil-- The doctor said memory loss is normal after a head injury, especially one like yours. It'll be back before you know it. Just give it some time."

Time. Right now time was all he had but something

inside of him, something deep, alerted him and made it seem that wasn't the case.

❄

*K*elsey left the hospital via the service elevator to avoid the gathering media reporters and walked several blocks away from the hospital before hailing a cab. She could've called JT's driver, Sheldon, to pick her up but the car would've only drawn more attention to her departure from the hospital and her arrival home. This way she had a better chance at dodging the press.

She needed a shower, coffee, and sleep. In other words—a "napaccino" as Amanda liked to say. Just enough sleep for the caffeine to kick in so she could go about like it was a regular day.

She lifted a hand to cover her yawn during the ride home, staring out the window at the city she loved. Devon's memory loss plagued her. She couldn't imagine how it must feel to wake up and not remember. How frightening and disorienting it would be to have a blank where answers should be.

She closed her eyes and smothered a groan.

What was she going to do regarding JT's health? It scared her. And her grandfather's insistence that Devon was from Yorkton *terrified* her. Death was inevitable, she knew that. But in a way, JT's mental departure was crueler than death. He was here, physically, but mentally her seventy-eight-year-old grandfather believed in Santa's workshop and an underground city. JT's mind obviously wasn't present in reality.

But what if it is real? What if it is like he said and it is all true?

Really? You think Santa's workshop is directly under you? Down there with the rats and the sewage?

Noting their location, she spoke up. "Drop me here, please."

They were a couple of blocks away from the penthouse but she had a pretty good idea of what awaited her outside of the bookstore.

Crisp air filled her lungs and she was grateful for the sunny winter day because she blended in with the other pedestrians wearing bulky coats, gloves, and toboggans hats as well as sunglasses.

She tucked her long, identifiable hair into her knit hat and rocked a cheap pair of oversized glasses with more scratches than visibility, and set off to blend in with the crowd. The low-key disguise allowed her to walk by the press gathered on every corner keeping their required distance away from the bookstore entrance, and she entered PAGES as though she was a customer.

Kelsey maintained her disguise and avoided her employees for the time being. Amanda was a fantastic, capable assistant manager, and until Kelsey got some sleep, the bookstore was in good hands. She needed some time to process things and attempt to come up with a plan.

It wasn't until she was inside the safety of the penthouse and greeted by Bronte that Kelsey released the breath she didn't realize she'd held.

"Ms. Kelsey, how is he?"

Kelsey turned to find Rita nearby. The housekeeper wrung her wrinkled hands at her waist, a worried expression on her face. Sheldon, her husband, stood behind her looking equally concerned. "He's sore and bruised, but awake and talking. He'll be fine, Rita. No worries."

"I was waiting for you to call me for pick up."

She nodded, knowing the couple was sincere in their desire to help. "I know, Sheldon, but the press knows JT's car, especially in this area. I walked right by them with no problems. Rita, would you make some coffee, please? I'm going to shower and take a quick nap."

"Of course. It will be waiting on you when you get out."

Kelsey murmured her thanks and made her way to her bedroom, feet dragging with every step and Bronte at her side.

She stripped down and took the hottest shower in recent memory, hoping the heat would help ease the tension in her neck and shoulders. Hair in a towel and wrapped in a thick robe, she made her way to the bed, thankful Rita had left a coffee mug on the bedside table.

Bronte left her position on the floor and hopped up on the bed by Kelsey's side. The dog snuggled close, as though to comfort, seemingly sensing something wasn't quite right. Other than a few business trips for book expos, it wasn't the norm for her not to be home overnight and Bronte stared at her with her big, brown doggy eyes, as though wanting to make sure nothing was wrong.

"What are we going to do, Bron? Hmm?" Kelsey shifted to lie down and Bronte adjusted her long frame to accommodate her without losing contact. Eyes closed, Kelsey filled her hands with Bronte's fluffy coat as she stroked the dog and soothed them both. "What are we going to do about JT?"

Chapter 13

Later that afternoon Kelsey exited the hospital elevator with her hands full. Her quick nap had turned into several hours, and the much-needed rest had gone a long way to refocus her.

The moment she turned the corner leading toward JT's room, she heard deep masculine laughter and couldn't stop the smile that formed. JT was definitely feeling better from the sound of it.

The hospital security guard ordered to stand outside JT's room was the same one from this morning and as she paused for an update, she handed him one of the coffees from the tray she carried. "Any visitors while I was gone, Paul?"

"Oh, thank you, Ms. Richards." Paul accepted the gift but looked uncomfortable.

"Uh-oh. Did something happen?"

"We had a few reporters up here who slipped by security downstairs, but they kept their distance when they saw me."

"But?"

"But there, uh, was also a lawyer."

"Mr. Wallingford's attorney?"

"No, ma'am. He came by, too, but this man was one of those guys from the TV commercials." The guard shifted his weight from foot to foot and tugged at the collar of his uniform. "My apologies, Ms. Richards, but he lunged by me and... got through the door."

"What?"

"No worries, Miss.. I got him, but it would've been a lot harder without Devon's help. Never seen anyone move that fast. He shoved the guy back out of the room and away from Mr. Wallingford in a second flat. Big guy, too, though not as big as Devon in there."

So Devon had protected JT again? "What happened after that?"

"Well, turns out the man was actually trying to see Devon. He, uh, wanted to advise Devon of his right to sue because of the injury he sustained in helping Mr. Wallingford that night."

"Of course he did." Kelsey inhaled and sighed. JT's money was such a blessing--and a curse. "Was anyone injured? Is Devon okay?"

"Yes, ma'am. He's fine. They're in there laughing about it now and the lawyer has been banned from the hospital. Security's watching for him and the hospital has called in more of us to help. A couple of extra men will be nearby at all times."

She'd bet the hospital loved the added expense for that but then she was quite sure JT's bill would reflect the cost. "Thanks for the update. Enjoy the coffee. You probably don't need the caffeine jolt after all of that excitement, though."

"Thank you, Miss. My shift is about to end but my replacement will take good care of you."

"Thank you, Paul." JT had always preached kindness to everyone, especially employees or staff, otherwise known as the gatekeepers. Be kind to them, show them you notice their work and sincerely appreciate it, and they'd be even more diligent in their duties. Right now they needed diligent security. This incident as proof of that. It indicated the need for private security, something that JT had put off all of these years despite multiple people who cared about him telling him he needed protection.

Paul pushed the door open for her and stepped back to give her room to carry JT's requested items inside. Coffee, the food order, a deck of cards--because as JT put it Devon had no memory and they'd need *something* to do, and the days' papers so that JT could get a sense of what needed to be done for damage control.

Requesting the newspapers was proof positive she was correct in her comment to Neil about JT not being able to handle negative press about his mental state. Which is why there were a few papers missing from the bag she carried. "Here you go," she said, trying to sound breezy and lighthearted despite the worry draining her. "And before you ask, JT, yes, you got extra carrots."

"Isn't she wonderful, Devon? My girl takes good care of me."

Kelsey smiled at the praise and set about unbagging the food for the three of them. "I heard you had some excitement while I was gone."

"Nothing the guard and Devon couldn't handle, my dear."

"Still, Devon could've fallen getting up so fast, especially after this morning." She held Devon's gaze and tried to ignore the flutter in her stomach.

But a flutter of what? Excitement? Interest?

Devon looked better rested, had more color than the first time she'd seen him. He appeared to be freshly showered, too, his short hair atop his head still damp.

"Thanks for the rescue, by the way."

"Rescue? I thought you were the one going around rescuing people, Devon," Neil said from behind them.

Kelsey bit back a groan of unease. She'd managed to avoid Neil the entire day by leaving the hospital and sleeping through his texts, but here he was.

"A dizzy spell this morning after I stood up. Kelsey walked in during it and helped me back to bed."

"I see."

Neil gave her a look that almost made her think he was jealous.

Doesn't matter now.

She pulled herself away from the path her mind had taken and watched as Neil walked to where Devon sat and used a penlight to check his eyes.

"Anything since the dizzy spell this morning when Kelsey caught you? Weakness, nausea?"

"No."

"Flashes of memory?"

"No."

"How's the headache?"

"Tolerable."

Kelsey watched as Neil clicked off the light and stuck it back in his smock pocket, freeing his hands to lift the bandage on Devon's head.

"Good. Especially considering the reports I'm hearing about your antics today."

"Devon can handle himself," JT said. "He's proven that multiple times."

Neil seemed satisfied with his examination and stepped back from Devon, turning to face her and JT.

"That he has. Smells good in here."

Neil didn't wait for her to offer him a bite. He simply grabbed one of the spare forks and helped himself to the plate of food in front of her and the only meal she'd managed to eat--almost eat--today.

Kelsey glanced at JT and saw him eyeing Neil with irritation but what was she supposed to do? Pull the plate away? "Busy day?"

"Mmm, yes. Surgeries all day. Just got out and I'm starving."

"Kelsey's hungry, too," JT interjected. "She's been running ragged and only just settled down to *her* meal."

Neil took another bite--one more--than grabbed a napkin to wipe his mouth. "Mmm. So good. You know how much I love that place. Couldn't help myself."

"Yeah, that seems to be a characteristic of yours."

She'd sat opposite JT on the bed by his legs during Neil's examination of Devon, and now slid her hand from her lap to discreetly pinch JT to remind him to behave. But, positioned where he was in the chair beside of JT's bed, Devon apparently saw the move and winked at her from behind the hand he'd lifted to cover his grin.

She wasn't sure how much time Devon and JT had spent together before she arrived but anyone in JT's presence quickly surmised *he* was a character who often couldn't be contained.

Neil was oblivious to the undercurrent and, after another wipe at his mouth, wadded the napkin and lifted it over his head to shoot it toward the trashcan like a basketball. Other than a pointed glare in JT's direction, Neil let the comment slide.

"JT, how are you feeling?"

Kelsey hoped JT remembered what was at stake before saying something else he shouldn't.

"I'd be better off at home. You going to release me?"

"Actually, that's why I'm here." Neil turned to look at Kelsey, holding her gaze instead of JT's. "I've managed to perform a miracle. You're scheduled for release tomorrow morning." Kelsey's expression must have revealed her surprise because Neil nodded.

"Really? That's fantastic." So Neil and the hospital board had given up on trying to hold her grandfather for an evaluation?

"I thought you might like that," Neil murmured. "There are conditions that must be met but I assured the board it wouldn't be a problem for us."

Us?

Unease filled her at Neil's use of the word and she fought off the trepidation that threatened to sour her pleasure at the news. "What does that mean?"

"We should discuss that in private," Neil added.

Devon got to his feet. "I'll step out. But is there any news on my release before I go?" He pointed to the bandage on his head with one finger. "This is nothing, and I don't like taking up a bed someone else may need."

"Actually, Devon, I've arranged for you to stay on our long-term care floor."

Kelsey watched as Devon frowned.

"Why can't I leave?"

"Has your memory returned?" Neil asked. "Do you know where you live?"

Devon's reluctance to admit the truth was palpable. "No."

"Then under the circumstances I think we'd all agree staying here is better than roaming the streets in the cold, don't you?"

"Don't be ridiculous. There's no sense in Devon staying in the hospital if he's well enough to leave, and Kelsey and I have already discussed this. Devon's coming home with us."

"Excuse me?" Neil's gaze narrowed on JT before shifting to her.

Kelsey sucked in a sharp breath. From the frying pan into the fire...

"Kelsey, you agreed to this?"

"Of course she did," JT countered. "I know Devon. The man saved my life. If he's fit enough to be released, the least I can do is give him a place to stay until his memory returns."

Kelsey divided her attention among JT and Neil and Devon, all of whom looked to be in a battle of wills, for dominancy. And all of them stared at her as though waiting for her to take their side.

"Devon, I need to talk to JT and my fiancée alone. Please step outside."

Chapter 14

"**E**x- fiancée," JT interjected before she had a chance to protest the title.

Kelsey fought the urge to roll her eyes and remind JT that the medical release Neil had just provided could be taken away in a heartbeat.

Devon moved toward the door and, even though it wasn't the time for such thoughts, she wondered how someone of his height and stature was so stealthy. But maybe that came with the job title of "security"?

Devon paused at the door and turned to face them.

"I'll admit I would rather be anywhere else but a hospital, and I don't want to intrude, JT."

"Nonsense, boy. It's no intrusion at all."

Neil shifted his weight and crossed his arms over his chest. "I don't blame Devon for not wanting to stay in the hospital but perhaps putting him up in a hotel would be a better solution. Right, Kelsey?"

She opened her mouth to agree but made the mistake of looking at JT. Holding his gaze, she couldn't form the words because JT's request for time with

Devon resounded silently in her head along with JT's promise to behave himself.

"Bah. Why bother with a hotel when we have plenty of room? And why wouldn't I want my security close to me after the mess I've caused? I owe the boy. It's my fault he's injured in the first place."

Neil looked as surprised as she felt at JT's declaration.

"Devon is your security? As in bodyguard?"

JT scoffed at Neil's suspicious query. "Of course. Who'd you think he was? Look at the boy. I know I may have been a little confused earlier but I'm not now. You've both been giving me grief about hiring protection. I would've thought you'd seen him for what he is even though I was out of my head."

"Kelsey, you knew about this?"

She swallowed hard and studied JT. "We've discussed security many times in recent months, yes."

"And you were aware that JT hired Devon?" Neil pinned her with his stare, waiting on a response.

"What a question. Of course she wasn't, otherwise she would've told you who he was last night." JT nodded to confirm his words. "She's been so busy at the bookstore I hadn't even told her I was interviewing, much less had hired someone."

Devon remained at the door and she studied him, trying to gauge his reaction to their news.

Could it be true? Was that the connection between Devon and JT? The *real* connection?

It made sense. Perfect sense, actually.

She and JT *had* discussed security on numerous occasions, because of JT's late night comings and goings for business deals, and because of the state of the world today, along with his age and health. But why was this only coming to light now?

"Exactly how long has Devon worked for you?" Neil asked.

"Not long. A few days. I only just hired the boy. Glad I did, though. I'm sorry, son," JT said to Devon, shaking his head. "I'm not at all happy about you getting hurt but I'm grateful you were there when I needed you. It's not easy for an old man to admit he's not the man he used to be. I didn't want to give into the harping because it meant it was true, but I couldn't have handled those thugs without you."

"Why didn't you tell me this earlier?" Devon asked. "I've been in here for the last hour and you haven't said anything about me working for you."

"You told me the doc wanted you to remember things on your own. I thought it'd be best if you did but with Neil here trying to keep you in the hospital on a technicality, it's time to speak up, don't you think?"

Once again all three men turned to look at her and she faltered under the weight of their stares. She wasn't sure what to make of JT's announcement but she welcomed it with open arms. JT's gaze was clear and all hint of confusion nowhere in sight. "Well, there you have it. Mystery solved."

Neil straightened to his full height. "No offense, Devon, but I'd still like privacy to discuss some things with JT and Kelsey."

"Of course."

Neil walked to the door and waited for Devon's departure, shutting the door after him with a decisive *click* of sound.

Kelsey watched Neil, able to tell he barely held onto his patience.

"Kelsey, you can't seriously consider allowing JT to take Devon home with you," Neil said.

"Why's that?" JT demanded.

"Why? You're asking me *why*? You just said he's a new hire. You know nothing about that man. He could be dangerous."

"Who says I don't know anything about him?"

"What's his last name?"

"Oh, bosh. A man is more than his name and just because he can't recall it at the moment doesn't make Devon a criminal."

"Fine. Maybe he doesn't remember, but what about you? What's his last name?"

"It's... Give me a minute," JT said, rubbing his head. "York. That's it. Devon York."

"You're sure?"

"Why wouldn't I be?"

"Oh, I don't know," Neil said, "maybe because you weren't sure of anything a matter of hours ago?"

"Well, I'm sure now. I know I talked out of my head before, but I think Devon's name just reminded me of that story I used to tell Kelsey, and I got confused. As you keep telling me, I'm getting *old*."

Neil glanced at Kelsey and she shrugged, nodding her head. "It makes sense."

"Course it does. And as for Devon being released, it's my home and as such, you don't have the right to tell me who I can or can't host."

Feeling like a volcano was about to erupt between the two dominant men, Kelsey cleared her throat. "JT, Neil is simply voicing a legitimate concern. It's understandable given the suddenness of this revelation of yours after what happened last night, don't you think?"

"He has his own agenda, my dear. Don't mistake his words for something they're not."

"I went to bat for you against the hospital board," Neil argued, pacing across the room. "If not for my love for Kelsey, you would be sitting in a padded room right now."

"Neil!" Really? *That* was his bedside manner?

"Well, thankfully I came to my senses before you let them use you like a puppet," JT said, glaring back at Neil.

Kelsey stood, unable to sit there a second longer. "Stop it! *Both* of you."

"Yeah? Well, you just proved there's a reason for concern that has nothing to do with you talking crazy and everything to do with the fact that this is New York. Taking a total stranger into your home is nothing short of lunacy. Especially one built like a tank."

"Who'd hire a weak little wimp to protect them? What good would that do? He's security. Of course he's been checked out."

"And you can provide proof?"

"You got a warrant? Privacy laws and non-disclosures mean I can't just go around showing people Devon's business, not to mention my own."

Neil lifted his hands in the air in obvious frustration. "Forget it. I'm not having this argument. I'm going to go to the head of the board to tell them I think a mandatory psych evaluation *is* a good idea."

"No!" Kelsey rushed around Neil and stood between him and the door. "Neil, you can't do that."

"Why not?"

"Because... Because I would never forgive you."

Neil's expression tightened even more but she saw his anger cooling in small degrees.

"Kelsey, my dear, do not encourage his foolishness. He's just being a bully."

She ignored JT and moved toward Neil, every step harder than the one before it. "Neil... If you do that and they… You *can't* take JT away from me."

A part of her hated herself for giving Neil this edge and power over her but it couldn't be helped. Despite JT's sudden announcement regarding Devon's identity, her grandfather was still under close scrutiny and would undoubtedly remain so. She'd do whatever it took to protect JT.

Neil ran a hand through his thick hair and mussed it but he still looked like the handsome, sexy doctor with whom she'd fallen so in love. The one passionate about his work and his patients. She needed to remember *that* side of him. Not the side so angry right now that he'd let pride and anger decide JT's fate.

"Kelsey, I wouldn't be able to live with myself if you got hurt." Neil lifted his hand and indicated the door with a wave.

As upset as she was with Neil's behavior, his gaze told the sincerity of his words. He meant it.

Maybe their relationship hadn't been perfect but they'd shared so much. And in his own way, she was sure Neil did love her. Just like she loved him. Feelings like that didn't just disappear because of a breakup.

"I understand. I do, and I appreciate your concern. But if JT says Devon is trustworthy then it's true. Neil, it's just for a few days. Devon can lounge around the penthouse until his memory returns and then go home. Everything will then go back to normal."

"Kelsey, he doesn't have to stay with you. Besides, if Devon is an employee, why not have JT's attorney look at those records, find out where Devon lives, and let him recover there? Hire a nurse for him if it makes you feel better."

"That boy took a bullet for me and as such he's *my* responsibility," JT said, his tone rough with emotion. "The least I can do is keep an eye on him and not leave him to fend for himself with a stranger."

"For the love of-- You can barely take care of your-self," Neil argued. "The photos in the papers are proof of that."

She lifted her hand and placed it on Neil's arm, drawing his attention even though she didn't say a word. A muscle worked in Neil's clenched jaw as he held her gaze for a long moment. Finally he released a sound of frustration but nodded.

"Fine. Fine, I'll release JT and Devon tomorrow, but the board's requirement that I visit JT for daily exams stands. I'll stop by every evening after work to check on them--and you."

Neil stepped close and used the hand she'd placed on his arm to pull her even closer, brushing his lips across her cheek.

"I love you, Kelsey. I hope you see that now."

Chapter 15

The following morning, Devon waited for the nurse to leave his room before tossing back the thin sheet and moving to the closet to retrieve his clothes. According to the nurse, his release paperwork was being processed and he wanted to be ready to leave the moment he was able.

On the one hand he understood JT wanting to make sure he was cared for in appreciation of his help. As his employer it was just good business. But on the other hand...

Based on JT and Kelsey's responses, neither of them knew enough about him to be inviting him into their home.

Hopefully JT had performed a thorough background check before hiring him, but the fact remained he could be anyone. A look in the mirror told him that. He might not remember who he was or where he was from but he knew he was in great physical shape and he'd now stepped up twice to protect JT.

According to them, you work for the guy. Isn't that reason enough?

He removed the scrub shirt, tossing it onto the bed before he shucked his hospital-issued pants and shoved his feet into the slacks he'd worn when admitted. He'd yanked them up over his hips, just as the door to his room opened.

"Oh!"

Buttoned and zipped, he turned to find Kelsey standing awkwardly in the doorway, head and eyes averted. "Hey. Good morning."

"Good, ummm… I didn't look. I mean, well, I guess I did, but I didn't *see* anything. It was more that I realized what you were *doing* rather than actually seeing…."

"It's not a problem. I'm dressed. Come in." He held the black shirt from the hospital bag his hand. "Have they been in to see JT yet?"

"Yes. The administrator just left after having JT sign off on the paperwork. Um, once everything is done JT's driver will meet us downstairs. You can, um, wait in JT's room until then if you like. I brought in some coffee and breakfast sandwiches. There's plenty. And-- Oh, here. These are for you."

Devon accepted the garment bag but made no move to open it. "What's this?"

"A fresh shirt and a coat. Sorry, but I didn't get pants. I wasn't sure of your size but I think those should work. Once we get home I'll call and have some slacks and whatever else you think you may need delivered."

He wanted to argue the kindness but he felt the blood crusted in the material of the shirt he still held. "I'll reimburse JT."

"Think nothing of it."

"I'll reimburse JT," he said again. "He's already paid for my medical bills."

"Which is why a few shirts and the like are nothing in the scheme of things," Kelsey argued, her tone soft but firm. "Devon, really. Please let JT--me--do this for you. He's all I have in the world and I don't want to think about what could've happened had you not been there that night."

It seemed petty to refuse when she put it like that, so he tossed the ruined shirt aside and unzipped the bag. Inside was a lightweight gray pullover and a black wool coat. "Thank you. These look nice."

"You're welcome."

Awkward silence filled the air until he realized he should probably put the shirt on and set about getting it off of the hanger. "Kelsey... Are you sure you're comfortable with me staying with you and your grandfather?"

After donning the shirt, he left the coat still bagged on the bed and grabbed his boots.

"Of course. It's only for a little while."

Devon smirked and shook his head, lifting his gaze to lock on hers. "That last statement says a lot."

"Oh, I mean..."

"Hey, it's okay. This is an odd situation. But if I'm JT's security, I'd be remiss in my job if I didn't warn you against taking in a complete stranger, and right now that's what I am. The doc is right about that."

Kelsey pulled the garment bag over to where she stood, removing the coat and laying it neatly atop his bed.

"JT has always been a good judge of character, whether in his personal life or business dealings. He has a discernment I'd give anything to possess and could have used many times over the years. He believes in you and I believe in JT so... yes, I'm okay with you staying with us."

He finished donning his boots and stood, watching the way her eyes widened just a tad as she took in his appearance.

Devon stared deep into her gray-green eyes, and slowly moved toward her, silently daring her to prove her words and not back away. He was highly pleased when she didn't. "I appreciate the vote of confidence but it doesn't sound like you're giving yourself enough credit."

She rolled her eyes and laughed. "Unfortunately, it's true. I'm a better at judging books and their success than I am at seeing people's motives."

"Or, maybe you see what they want you to see and give them the benefit of the doubt. You can't blame yourself for that. It just means you're a good person."

"Wow."

"What?"

She smiled and shook her head.

"Come on, what's that about?"

"You sounded a whole lot like JT just then."

"Ah, your grandfather seems like a good man."

"He's the best."

"Is your mom or dad as close to JT as you are?" The moment the question left his lips he knew he'd stepped onto a minefield. Her expression fell and the smile faded from her eyes.

"My parents are dead. They died when I was fourteen. Gram and JT raised me after that."

Devon silently kicked himself for ruining what had been a pleasant conversation. "I'm sorry. I didn't know. "

"No. No, it was a long time ago. Despite everything, I had a really great and adventurous childhood. Remind me to tell you about it some time."

Emotions flickered across her face, a mix of wistfulness and sadness, and he knew in that second she was somewhere else. "I will. But with a childhood like that, why the frown?"

"Hm? Oh, nothing. The last few days are catching up to me, I guess."

He lifted a hand and indicated the television. "I can understand why. JT's all over the news."

"That he is," she said wryly. "I keep hoping it will blow over but so far it hasn't."

Men with JT's wealth tended to have that sticking-power. "Kelsey... I don't remember why we were in that alley. Or why I didn't stop him from going there in the first place as his security detail, but I'm sorry for my part in this."

"Well," she said, amusement audible in her voice as she smiled, "obviously your memory *is* impaired if you think you could've controlled where JT goes or what he does."

"I've got my hands full as his body guard, huh?"

"Oh, yeah. You could say that."

The smile was back on her and he found himself unable to look away. "Anything else I should know about him that I've forgotten?"

"Are you asking if the reports are true?"

He waited, let the question hang there between them and watched her closely as she formed a response. The press had managed to track down someone who was at the scene that night, an EMT, who had described the old man's mutterings as "senseless" and "the ramblings of a crazy man."

"JT has some health issues," she finally murmured. "Neil believes they're beginning to impact JT in a variety of ways, one of which is possibly his cognition."

"Can't be easy hearing that."

"It's not. But Neil is an excellent doctor and something does appear to be going on with JT, but only time will tell."

Chapter 16

Good doctor or not, Devon knew the doc's interest and claim on Kelsey had been clear the moment the man stepped into JT's room last night, as had the doc's dislike of JT's insistence that Devon stay with them. He could only imagine what was said once he'd left the room. When he'd gone back to eat dinner the topics remained upbeat and impersonal. "Do you think that's why JT hired me? Because he knows he's... slipping?"

"I don't know. Possibly. I've certainly said enough to JT about protecting himself and hiring security so maybe because of the health issues, he finally decided to listen. It's possible."

"The television mentioned JT saying some odd things."

"Yes. JT was very... confused when the officials found the two of you. He apparently confused your last name and a story he used to tell me from my childhood and... It's a long story. But once your memory returns you can answer any remaining questions anyone may have about that night. In the meantime, maybe Neil can figure out what's going on with JT."

"Sounds like a plan." He stared at her, wanting to ask more questions but hesitant all the same.

"Devon, just say it. Whatever it is."

A low chuckle left his chest as he looked his fill of her, taking in her long hair and curvy frame. From all appearances she looked soft but having seen her stand up to JT and her ex, he knew she was made of stronger stuff. "Why did you and the doc break up?"

The question changed her before his eyes and wariness overtook her features. "That's really personal."

"So's watching me get dressed."

She gasped. "I *didn't!*"

"Mmm. Are you sure?" He watched her squirm and enjoyed her flustered state for a moment before chuckling. A bright flush rose into her cheeks and the added color made her even more beautiful. "I'm teasing you. As to the question, I'm asking so I know if there are other aspects I need to take into consideration when it comes to JT's security, like your breakup, or the doc. Is your ex someone JT can trust?"

"You need to know this even though you don't remember JT hiring you?"

He shrugged. "Seems to me my job means protecting JT from anyone bent on doing him--or those close to him--harm, whether I remember or not."

The tension between Kelsey, JT and the doc had been palpable last night. Even though Kelsey was right and he didn't remember JT hiring him, a job was a job. His gut told him the undercurrents he'd felt in JT's room were about more than just a breakup.

"I'm surprised you haven't seen photos of me and Neil scrolling across the television screen."

He had. But he wanted to hear what she had to say about her relationship with the doc firsthand and not the pieced together gossip portrayed as news.

Kelsey shoved her hair off of her face and avoided Devon's gaze.

"One of the tabloids caught Neil with another woman and printed some very... risqué photos of them. Neil says it was a set up, but whether it was or it wasn't, our breakup was messy and ugly and painful. And now you know what everyone else in New York and the world knows."

"I'm sorry that happened to you. I can't imagine going through something so personal while under a microscope." He really couldn't. People needed privacy at such times, not to have every aspect of their life made public to be played out before an audience.

Kelsey's long lashes lowered protectively over her eyes and he immediately felt the lack of connection. She intrigued him, made him want to know more about how she managed to seem so sweet in a world full of wolves.

"Is Neil trustworthy?" she murmured. "That's a good question. But I'm not sure of the answer. The hospital board is panicking because of JT's antics, and Neil is feeling... pressured."

She made it sound like the doc was between a rock and a hard place, but Devon couldn't help but think the good doc might be laying it on a little thick and using the situation to his advantage. "Have you actually talked to anyone on the board? Heard this from them personally?"

"No, but I'm sure they or their representatives will be in touch soon enough."

*D*espite JT's name and clout with the hospital it took a while to complete all of the release paperwork. Finally, Devon and JT were free to leave and a hospital security team escorted them, and Kelsey, out of the building. Sheldon, JT's driver and the housekeeper's husband, drove them to JT's home.

Devon watched as Kelsey stared out of the tinted windows of the vehicle, the tiny furrow between her eyebrows coming and going as her thoughts changed.

"What's got you frowning so, my dear?" JT asked from beside of her. "Tell me."

Devon waited along with JT for Kelsey's answer.

She turned away from the window and gave her grandfather a smile.

"I'm wondering if Rita can handle you while I'm at work."

Work? As in a job? He didn't imagine many women with Kelsey's social status would bother working, content to spend their days shopping or lunching or performing some endless array of charitable fundraisers.

JT chuckled and winced, pressing one hand to his side over his injured ribs.

"Oh, JT, are you sure you shouldn't have stayed another day or two?" she asked.

Considering the flash of pain he'd seen cross JT's face, Devon was concerned as well. When Devon had gone to JT's room to await official word of their release, JT had looked good, but now the elderly gentleman's forehead glistened with sweat and there was a tremor in his hands, no doubt due to pain.

"No, no. I'm fine. No need to hold up a bed--two beds. No worries. I feel better just knowing I'll soon be home."

The large car turned a corner and Kelsey glanced out the window once more.

"Still there. Legal by an inch at most," she muttered.

Devon leaned forward to see whatever it was she saw and spotted a group of photographers and television crews gathered on the sidewalks.

"That's home," she said to Devon, pointing. "The bookstore takes up the first couple of floors, and we're in the penthouse."

Devon studied the building and noted the evidence of construction taking place on the floors between, which would give access to strangers. He mentioned the problem aloud and JT nodded in approval of Devon's observation.

"I can put a hold on it for a short time," JT said.

Sheldon made another turn and drove the limo through a secured gate and once beneath the building, Kelsey exhaled, her mouth forming a small O.

Devon got out of the car and studied their surroundings. The parking garage was eerily empty, with only a handful of cars, mostly vintage, parked nearby.

"JT's," Kelsey murmured as she came to stand by his side.

"He's got good taste."

Devon and Sheldon helped JT exit the vehicle, and once JT was upright, Sheldon immediately positioned himself on JT's uninjured side for the short walk to the elevator. Sheldon kept pace with JT, the two older men's banter proving they were more than mere employer and employee.

Kelsey walked several steps ahead of them all.

"Kelsey, are you all right?"

"I'm fine," she said, never breaking her stride. "I just want to get inside."

"Kelsey doesn't like the press, Devon," JT said. "Hasn't since they were so insistent after her parents were killed."

Kelsey arrived at the elevator bank and turned. She met Devon's gaze briefly before looking away and lifting her shoulders in a shrug, jabbing the button with an unpolished fingernail.

"I was a child and they were relentlessly brutal. There's no excuse for that. I'm sorry, JT. I should've helped you."

"Nonsense. Walking slow doesn't require assistance. Sheldon's the one using me as a crutch to rest his old bones. Isn't that right?"

"Yessir."

Sheldon, a full thirty years younger than JT, winked at Kelsey and Devon saw her give the elegantly dressed driver a smile of warm thanks in return.

Devon had spent enough time in JT's room, either visiting or waiting to be released, to make some observations when it came to his employer and Kelsey, one of which was that, by all accounts, they were both genuinely nice people. Through the partially open door, he'd seen Kelsey give coffee to the guard outside JT's room, heard the thank yous and pleases expressed as IVs were refreshed and monitors checked.

They treated everyone with respect no matter the job they performed. In fact, the only person Devon had seen JT treat with any disrespect was Kelsey's ex. And after what she'd told him regarding her breakup with the doc, Devon could easily understand why.

The elevator dinged but didn't open and he watched while Kelsey entered a code on the keypad. Despite her obvious desire to be out of the range of paparazzi, JT's granddaughter stepped to the side and held the door while Sheldon helped JT shuffle on.

Once inside the elevator, JT leaned against the back wall and struggled to catch his breath. Devon followed Kelsey onto the lift and watched as she swiped a keycard over an electronic device and entered the six-digit code before pressing the PH button. "Have the codes been changed since the night of the mugging?"

Devon gained all of their attention with his question.

"Nothing's been changed," Kelsey said. "Does it need to be?"

"It's fine," JT said, his voice gruff. "Nothing needs changed."

"I know it can be a hassle but the cards would've been in our wallets the night of the mugging. Anything is hackable with the right person and equipment." Devon watched as JT frowned and shook his head once more.

"You didn't have a card yet and I wasn't carrying one that night."

"I'll see to it that George—the guard on the street level entrance—gets one for you," Kelsey said.

The elevator doors opened directly into the penthouse where a friendly bark greeted them. Devon tucked the name George into his memory for later.

"Hi, baby. Did you miss us?" Kelsey said to the dog

as she stepped out and waited for JT and Sheldon once more.

Other than a quick glance at the newcomer, the dog ignored Devon and followed her mistress, hugging Kelsey's side, her head lifted to watch Kelsey's every move with pure adoration.

"I'm guessing that's Bronte."

"You remembered."

Kelsey flashed him a smile that made his gut tighten in response, much like it had yesterday morning in the hospital when she'd wrapped her arm around his waist and led him back to bed. Yeah, he remembered.

He noticed more and more about Kelsey with every passing minute. Her beauty, her kindness, her smile.

Those eyes...

And if you're married?

Chapter 17

Once again, he pushed away any thought of Kelsey as more than JT's granddaughter. Regardless of whether he was married or involved with anyone, it was imperative he keep things professional.

JT's grunt filled the air as Sheldon helped settle his employer into a chair.

"I broke four ribs once," Sheldon told his employer. "Couldn't sleep anywhere but in a recliner for over a month. Rita had me move this from your den for the time being. It'll be easier for you to get up and down out of this chair."

"Thank you, Sheldon." JT wheezed from the exertion and settled back into his chair with a sigh. "Oh, yes. This will do quite nicely."

"I'll go let Rita know we're here in case she didn't hear us come up. I'm sure she'll have something cooked for you for lunch."

JT uttered his thanks, declined lunch, and attempted

to make himself comfortable. Sheldon left the room, and Devon studied the penthouse.

Instead of designer sleek, cold glass and steel, Kelsey and JT's penthouse felt cozy and homey. He imagined they spent their winter nights in front of the walled gas fireplace, each with a good book from the store downstairs.

Kelsey dropped her purse and at the sound, Devon shifted his focus to her. "You have a very beautiful home."

"It's all Kelsey's doing. Didn't move here until after her grandmother passed so she took on the task of making it a home for us."

Kelsey tossed her coat on the back of the couch before bending to pet her four-legged friend.

"Hello, my pretty girl. Bronte, this is Devon. Go say hello properly."

Bronte followed Kelsey's hand signal and padded straight to Devon. The dog sat at Devon's feet, gave him a long stare, and then lifted her paw to shake.

"Well, look at you. So formal." Devon greeted the dog by taking her paw and then gently patted her head. "You're a sweetheart, aren't you? And so soft."

"Isn't she great?"

Kelsey made no effort to hide her love of her pet or her interest in the exchange, and Devon had the feeling this meeting was about more than simply showing off a cute dog trick. Dogs were known to be good judges of character and it seemed as though he'd managed to pass the "Bronte Test."

JT groaned softly as he pressed a button and the recliner began to change shape, lifting the man's legs slowly while easing the back of the chair lower.

"JT?" Kelsey murmured, a deep frown pulling her eyebrows low.

"Shh. I'm fine, my dear. Right as rain. Just need to get comfortable and catch my breath."

"I wish you would've consented to us getting you a wheelchair."

"It would've only made me feel old. Now, go on. Sheldon and Rita can keep me company while you show Devon around. Son, make yourself at home."

"Thank you, sir." Devon shared the concern he read on Kelsey's face and hoped the doc hadn't released JT from the hospital too soon.

Kelsey leaned her hips against the side of the leather couch behind her, watching him as he scanned what he could see of the city. Devon felt her gaze on him like a physical touch. "You've got quite a view."

The building wasn't the tallest in the city by any means but it was in that particular neighborhood, and it had a spectacular view of a park. The impending dusk showcased the many streetlights and car lights, and from this high up, the snow made everything look pristine and perfect like….

A dizzying wave washed over him and an image appeared in his mind of a village coated in snow. Cold, crisp air blew white with every breath, and above his head sparkled stars in an inky black sky. He was outside. Standing on a hill above the tiny town, barely able to make out a light here and there.

The image faded as fast as it had appeared but the lightheadedness lingered for long moments afterward. Devon gripped the window frame to steady himself and took a few slow, deep breaths until his head stopped whirling.

"I knew from a young age that I would live in a pent-house," JT murmured from his chair. "I wanted to be in a high spot where I could see everything. Having a home like this was the top of my list."

Devon turned to face them, keeping his hand in place against the frame just in case.

"You had a bucket list?" Kelsey's expression was one of surprise.

"Oh, some people call it that but I've always thought of it more like a goal list. Or life list." Eyes closed, JT nodded. "It was a mighty fine day when I found this building and marked it off my list."

Kelsey regarded her grandfather with an expression of bemusement.

"You've purchased and sold a lot of buildings over the years, JT. What's special about this one?"

JT sighed and seemed to sink deeper into his chair.

"It just is."

"Well, I've never heard you mention this list. What else is on it?"

Devon watched as a brief smile perked up the corners of the old man's mouth, changing the shape of his white mustache and beard.

"Only a few things now, my dear. Only a few things. Let's get Devon settled, shall we? I doubt either one of us got any rest with the nurses coming in all hours of the day and night. I'd say Devon is a might tired too."

Devon met the old man's gaze and realized JT must have seen him grab hold of the window frame.

He knew for certain that was the case when JT pursed his lips and nodded at him.

Kelsey straightened from her perch against the couch, disturbing Bronte's position where she leaned against Kelsey's legs. JT's granddaughter approached the recliner and pressed a kiss onto the top of JT's balding head.

"Okay, but I want to know more about that list. I'll show Devon to his bedroom and be back to check on you in a little while."

"I'm fine. No need to rush."

It took Kelsey a long moment to pull her worried gaze away from JT but when she did, she tilted her head toward the opposite end of the room.

"Follow me."

Kelsey led the way across the wide living room. Bronte's nails clicked softly on the floor as the dog padded along behind her mistress and Devon fell into step behind them both, following them down a hall. "This is the guest area. Here is the home gym," she said, indicating a closed door with a wave of her hand. "The billiards room and den," she said, moving on. "This other hall leads to my room and JT's, but your room is here, at the end."

Kelsey opened a door and entered, and he found himself following her into a large, elegantly appointed room decorated in various shades of cream and gray with touches of black and red. A king-size bed hugged the wall opposite floor-to-ceiling windows.

From what he'd seen of the entry, dining and living rooms, the penthouse had been designed to take advantage of every possible view and this room was no exception. "This is really nice. Thank you."

"You're welcome. The, uh, bathroom is this way." She headed for a door and lit the interior. "All of the towels and whatever else you might need are in here. Oh, and your clothes closet is there," she said, pointing to another door. "But until we can get you a couple changes of clothes, I guess that's useless information."

Devon leaned his shoulder against the wall and stared at her. "You seem nervous. Because of me staying here?"

"No, I'm...."

He held her gaze. "Whatever it is you can say it."

"Okay. I will." She tucked her chin towards her chest and seemed to brace herself, straightening to her full height. "My grandfather is a good man."

"I think that's pretty obvious. Not everyone would be so quick to pay for medical bills or bring an employee home with them. But that's not why you're pointing it out, is it?"

"Devon, you seem like a nice guy. You do. Just... promise me you won't try to take advantage. It's blatantly obvious JT isn't at his best right now."

"Ah, I get it." Kelsey's expression was all too easy to read but her concerns were legitimate and not something to be dismissed lightly. "You're afraid I'm going to sue him. Get everything I can get because of this?" He indicated the bandage. "Is that it?"

Kelsey crossed her arms over her front and hugged herself. "I hope not. But it wouldn't be the first time someone's.... People like JT-- people who still have a heart for those around them--make for very vulnerable targets."

"As are the people who love him."

Kelsey stiffened at the statement and Devon knew he'd hit a nerve. One no doubt raw and exposed because of Neil's treatment of her. And maybe others? He couldn't imagine it was easy growing up in JT's shadow, and there were plenty of people far too willing to take a chance to get what they could.

In the way Kelsey had questions about her grandfather's list, Devon had questions about her life. The few she'd already answered only made him want to know more.

"I'm just saying money tends to bring out the worst in people."

Devon straightened and ignored the ache in his head caused from the bright lights shining in the bathroom. "Look, Kelsey, I don't know what's going on in that beautiful head of yours and I can only imagine who has hurt you and all the various ways they've done it, but I do not mean you or JT any harm. If you'd rather me not stay here…."

"No. I'm sorry."

"Don't be sorry."

"But I am. I'm making you feel unwelcome and that's not my intent. I just-- I'm tired and worried about JT and Neil."

"I understand."

"You do? Would you mind explaining it to me then?"

A smile caught him off guard but he didn't try to stop it from forming. He shifted, moved until he stood within touching distance, and reached out to lightly brush a stray strand of her long blond hair off of her cheek. "You love your grandfather and don't want anyone or anything to hurt him." He lowered his hand to his side. "It's pretty simple. What's not to understand about that? I would be on guard, too. You're wise to question me."

Without thought, Devon used his thumb to touch his ring finger on his left hand, right at the base. No wedding ring. No tan line or indentation, which meant the odds were he hadn't worn one before the mugging took place.

But that didn't mean he was single and right now he was in serious danger of crossing an important boundary.

Protectiveness was attractive on her. So was her beauty, her grace, and her loving nature.

But if his job was to protect JT, and thereby protect Kelsey, the last thing he could do was cross the line between professional and personal because doing so could cost them their very lives.

"That sounds like sage advice coming from a man with no memory."

———————————

Chapter 18

———————————

"*That sounds like sage advice coming from a man with no memory.*"

What was it about her comment that bugged him? Devon spent the rest of the afternoon and early evening sitting in the luxurious penthouse keeping JT company while Kelsey disappeared downstairs to check in on her bookstore.

As tired as he was of lying in bed, Devon knew not to push himself too fast or else risk falling on his face. The dizziness earlier had reminded him that he wasn't in top shape, if his lack of memory and bruised temple weren't proof enough.

The lingering headache from his injury came and went throughout the day like a wave. If he moved too fast the room had a tendency to tilt but so long as he took his time, he wasn't grabbing furniture to steady himself.

He and JT watched some television while Bronte dozed on the floor. Sheldon and his wife hovered over them and it wasn't long before JT told them both to go home. Rita had made enough food to feed an army, and as they were in for the night, Sheldon wouldn't be driving them anywhere.

Devon noted that neither the housekeeper nor driver looked happy about the idea of leaving JT. No doubt Kelsey had requested they keep a closer-than-normal eye on JT due to his behavior, but JT overruled their protests.

Not long after the older couple departed, JT fell asleep in his recliner. After a bit of dozing himself, Devon awoke and shoved himself slowly to his feet, earning a lazy head-lift from Bronte.

The dog watched Devon's movements and didn't seem too concerned until Devon approached the opening leading to the rear of the penthouse. Bronte's nails made a clicking noise when she quickly got up to follow. "Afraid I'll steal something or are you getting hungry, too?"

His stomach had started to growl during the last half-hour of the old western JT wanted to watch. He hoped he wasn't overstepping, but Kelsey and JT had both said to make himself at home, and it felt better to be productive than to sit there.

Carefully marked containers listing the contents and heating instructions filled the fridge. He poked around for a bit and finally chose Pesto Chicken Florentine and Spinach Tomato Tortellini, then set about reheating dinner for three.

A little while later, Bronte lifted her head from atop her paws and bounded out of the room.

Devon sliced freshly warmed bread when Kelsey

appeared, a curious frown marring her beautiful features.

"There you are."

"Hey. I hope you don't mind."

"No complaints from me, but you are supposed to be resting. Where are Rita and Sheldon?"

"JT sent them home and told them to keep the regular schedule because he, uh, didn't want them 'hovering like hummingbirds'."

Kelsey set her lips in a firm line, confirming Devon's earlier belief she'd asked the couple to watch over them. "I take it they're not here all of the time?"

"No. Rita comes in a few days a week to clean and cook. She has auto-immune issues and can't work full-time because too much will send her into a flare up. Sheldon is on call for JT as needed, though."

She moved to the sink and washed her hands.

"You've been gone a while. Everything okay downstairs?"

"Yeah, mostly. There were a couple of large orders that needed sorted out due to an employee mistake, and then a reporter snuck into my office..."

Devon dropped the knife and quickly moved to where she stood at the sink, gently turning her to face him. "Are you okay?"

Kelsey stared up at him, a smile teasing the corners of her mouth as she plucked up a towel and dried her hands.

"I'm fine. The man's made himself a problem before but he actually wore a disguise to get past my employees. I had a quick meeting with everyone and I think they'll be more diligent now."

Devon wanted to argue her statement but chose to let it drop for the time being. A meeting wouldn't fix a lack of security, and the antics of the press wouldn't change until JT's behavior became old news. He would take a look around tomorrow, make sure Kelsey had the security she needed, and talk to JT if she didn't.

He wasn't sure what plan of action had been established for Kelsey or her business security-wise, but Devon knew JT would want it covered for her protection.

After waking up in the hospital, he hadn't been able to remember what he did for a living but now that he knew, now that it was necessary in order to protect Kelsey, it was like his mind opened a vault and allotted him details pertinent to his vocation. Logistics flooded his mind, readily available for access.

"Devon? What's wrong?" Kelsey's voice sharpened. "Did you just remember something?"

He blinked to awareness. Kelsey's hand gripped his forearm, her fingers cold from when she'd washed them. "Yeah, in a way. I thought of security measures that might be necessary for you downstairs, ways to protect JT, and things just appeared. Like a computer download."

"That's *wonderful*."

Her smile drew his attention to her full lips. He searched his mind and fought the frustration buffeting him. "I still don't remember the important things, like my name and address." *If he was involved with anyone.*

"Well, it's a start. That means you're healing. It's only been forty-eight hours and you're all ready remembering some things. It's great progress, Devon. I'm happy for you."

She gave him a sideways hug that didn't last nearly as long as he would've liked. "Thanks."

"Come on. Let's get this finished so we can celebrate."

Chapter 19

Devon went back to work slicing the bread and Kelsey opened cabinets and pulled out plates and glasses. He finished the task and looked up to see her hiding a yawn behind her hand. "You're exhausted."

"Oh, sorry. That was rude."

"Rude? You've been at the hospital with JT and then went straight to work once we got here. You're allowed to be tired."

"I am, I admit it. I'll turn in early, after I get JT settled. I usually take Bronte out for her walk around 9 or so, but tonight I think I'll see if Carlos can do it since Sheldon is home for the night."

"Carlos?"

"A doorman from across the street. Things are pretty slow this time of night and he has a baby girl on the way so he can use the extra cash. He's done some errands for us when Sheldon isn't around."

Devon tucked the name back for future reference.

"If he can't do it I'll take Bronte out. The reporters won't recognize me... What?"

That smile again. A shake of her head. "Nothing. I'm just not used to having someone ask about my day or offer to help with Bronte other than JT."

"The doc doesn't help?" He regretted the question as he watched her expression become guarded once again and lifted his hands, palm up. "None of my business. Sorry."

Boundaries he reminded himself.

"I'm going to go set the table."

He watched Kelsey leave the kitchen but her response told Devon everything he needed to know. Stupid men didn't care enough about the women in their lives to talk to them, listen, and pitch in where needed. Apparently the doc fell into that category.

But thanks to his memory loss, he couldn't be sure where he fell on the scale when it came to such things. What he did know after the forty-eight hours he'd officially known Kelsey was that she fascinated him. In that short amount of time he'd seen her happy, sad, worried, exhausted, argumentative. He liked that she didn't try to hide her emotions. His gut told him that she wasn't a game player.

In short order the table was ready, drinks poured, and Kelsey had helped JT out of the recliner and to the table to eat his dinner.

They discussed the latest book craze drawing customers into her store when a loud buzz sounded. Kelsey excused herself and left the dining room to go to the console left of the elevator doors.

"Yes?"

"Good evening, Ms. Kelsey. Doctor Karev is here to see you," the security guard stated.

"Don't let him in," JT said, wagging his finger at her. "I've had enough of Neil for quite some time."

Devon silently agreed with JT about Kelsey's ex but kept his opinion to himself. He watched as she took a moment to compose herself and squared her shoulders.

"Buzz him in, please, Michael. Thank you."

Another name to remember. Devon added it to the growing list of those involved in keeping Kelsey and JT safe. After a good night's sleep he would make a point to introduce himself.

"Michael is one of the entry guards," JT said to Devon. "We're the only ones in the building except Kelsey's bookstore employees and construction workers remodeling the middle floors."

An entire building to themselves? In New York City?

Devon couldn't imagine the wealth required for such a thing. He digested the information and watched as Kelsey waited for her ex to arrive, noting the way she'd gone from relaxed and animated chatting about the Christmas novel soon to be made into a movie, to tense and stiff, silent.

Devon pushed his food around on his plate.

It was strange to feel so protective of people he barely knew, but he did. He didn't need his memory to know Kelsey and JT were unique compared to their peers. They genuinely cared about people. It was obvious from their behavior. But that wasn't the issue. The issue was the doc's worthiness of them, and based on what Devon had seen on the news and gleaned from Kelsey and JT's own statements, the doc was someone needing to be watched.

The elevator doors opened and Neil stepped off, a heavy, black trench coat flapping in his wake like a cape. Image was important to the doc, that much was obvious.

And who better to complete his image of successful neurosurgeon than to be dating a billionaire's granddaughter?

"Neil. What are you doing here?"

"Making a nuisance of himself, that's what," JT murmured only loud enough for Devon to hear.

The doc looked insulted by her query and his expression was enough to make Kelsey contrite. Devon's fingers tightened around his fork to the point of pain. She had no need to feel sorry.

"That was rude of me," she said. "Of course you're here to see your patients. I'm sorry, I wasn't thinking."

"You're overwhelmed. It's too much for you to deal with on top of everything else. I knew it would be," the doc murmured.

Devon bit back a comment best left unsaid by lowering his fork and grabbing his glass for a long drink, watching as the doc sauntered toward her until he was able to grasp Kelsey by the arms and hold her still while he bussed a kiss across her lips.

"You're going to shatter that glass if you squeeze it any harder, son."

Once again JT's comment was only for Devon's ears but the old man made his point. Devon loosed his white-knuckled grip on the water glass he'd emptied just to occupy himself during their exchange.

"I'm here now," the doc continued. "I'm not leaving your side until we've figured this mess out."

"Neil, I'm not—I'm fine. *Stop* making a fuss. I'd just forgotten you were supposed to check on them."

Kelsey's words sounded slightly slurred, like she uttered them through clenched teeth. Devon made the observation with interest and more than a little amusement.

"Yes, well, I'll always make a fuss over you, sweetheart."

Devon resisted the urge to roll his eyes and give voice to the comment he'd suppressed earlier.

"We're having dinner," Kelsey said.

"So I see," Neil said, looking in their direction to acknowledge them for the first time. "Gentlemen."

The good doctor held out his arm to escort Kelsey back to the table but Kelsey seemed to not notice and walked ahead of her ex.

Devon smirked at the sight and jumped up to pull out her chair but battled a wave of dizziness, no doubt payback for the spike of satisfaction he'd felt at her giving the doc the brush-off. He had to hold onto his chair for balance until the spots faded from in front of his eyes.

The doc seated Kelsey.

"You shouldn't be making any sudden moves, Devon."

Devon acknowledged the man's warning with a nod, angry with himself and at the weakness he'd just shown. Apparently he could add prideful to the growing list of qualities he was learning about himself since waking up with no memory. "Duly noted. Doesn't happen all the time though." Man, but he sounded defensive and didn't mean to.

"Neil," JT said in a grumbling tone. "I don't approve of you using us as an excuse to get back into Kelsey's good graces. That's not very gentlemanly of you."

Neil stiffened at JT's rebuke but casually seated himself beside of Kelsey with a nod toward her grandfather.

"What I'm doing is a courtesy for you, JT. Kelsey knows how I feel about her and we've discussed our breakup privately, as such matters require. She's agreed to work things out."

Kelsey gasped.

"Is that true?" JT's face darkened to a ruddy hue.

"I agreed to *talk*, JT. Neil is simply... hopeful."

Devon watched as Kelsey sent the doc a quelling glare, and her ex's jaw tightened before he flashed his pretty-boy smile at her.

"That I am. And why wouldn't I be? Now that the lines of communication are open, we'll work things through and be back together in no time. It's as good as done," he said, lifting his hand to brush his fingers against Kelsey's cheek. "But, if my visits to the pent-house upset you, JT, I'd be happy to escort you back to the hospital to receive care."

"Neil, stop it."

The doc clamped his mouth shut and sent a frus-trated glare in Kelsey's direction.

Devon leaned an elbow on the table and rubbed his mouth with his hand, watching the scene play out.

The doc definitely used JT's health in an attempt to worm his way back into Kelsey's life but it was becoming fairly obvious Kelsey was prepared to stand her ground. And why wouldn't she? The stakes were even on both sides. Where Neil held JT's healthcare in his pocket, Kelsey held their breakup and Neil's desire to reconcile in hers.

"You haven't worked things out *yet*. And now that

I've come to my senses you don't have a reason to put me in a hospital," JT stated.

"That remains to be seen. You still haven't explained why you were going out there dressed as you were." Neil plucked a piece of bread from Kelsey's plate, once again helping himself without asking.

Devon watched the interchange, his blood pressure rising on JT's behalf because of the doc's persistent threat.

JT, Kelsey, and the doc were in a personal battle that had nothing to do with him. But as someone hired to protect JT, Devon considered the doc a legitimate threat to his employer's well-being. Did the doc want JT committed? To what end? Kelsey wasn't his wife and Devon had a feeling if the doc pushed too hard, Kelsey would retreat once again. Was it just a power trip on the doc's part?

"I have my reasons, none of which are any of your concern."

Chapter 20

Neil straightened to his full height and glared at JT, and Devon watched the battle brewing.

"It is my concern when you were seen trying to drag Devon into the underground."

"I was confused. We've been over this already." JT wiped his mouth with his napkin with more force than necessary. "Neil, it's getting late and we've all had a long day. You should go."

"I'm sure you and Devon are tired, but it's still early yet. Kelsey, maybe you'd like to join me for dessert? We can go get our usual and let the patients get some rest."

"She hasn't finished eating and can't when you keep taking food from her plate," JT all but growled.

Devon watched the play of emotions cross Kelsey's face and wanted to slug the doc. The man was pushing hard to reconnect while he had the chance and he wasn't putting Kelsey's well-being first.

"I'm sorry, Neil, but I'm tired. The last few days have been exhausting, and I need to clean up before I go to bed."

"You pay a housekeeper for that."

Kelsey blinked and tilted her head to one side as she regarded her ex. "Maybe so, but I won't abuse her by making her job harder than it is."

Neil looked more than a little disgruntled by Kelsey's defense of the woman and tugged at the cuff of his pressed shirt.

"A rain check then. I won't take no for an answer."

Devon exchanged a glance with JT and knew the older man was having as hard of a time keeping his mouth shut.

"Yes. Some other time."

Devon stood slowly, more carefully this time, and gathered up his plate and utensils. "Excuse me while I carry these in. Doc..."

Devon didn't wait to see if the man acknowledged his exit but made his way through the penthouse into the kitchen and over to the sink. Frustration nipped at him because of what he'd just witnessed but as one of the "hired help" his hands were tied.

Kelsey was walking along on a tightrope and, at the moment, she was the only one who could get herself to the other side. Her grandfather's ramblings and odd behavior the night of the mugging had given Kelsey's ex the ammunition needed to ensure her cooperation. At least for the time being.

Whereas he… He was the reason the old man had gotten hurt. Because despite the bullet wound, he should've done a better job at protecting JT. Why hadn't he kept the man from going out there that night? Planted other guards in the vicinity to ward off potential danger like the thugs who'd mugged them? Persuaded JT to stop his nocturnal journeys all together?

Had Kelsey considered those facts? Had the doc already pointed them out to her?

He inhaled and released his aching grip on the glossy countertop, unable to acknowledge the twitch inside of him as jealousy because it would be highly unprofessional.

But that's exactly what it was. Jealousy--because the doc out there sitting beside Kelsey, trying so hard to suck her back into a relationship already knew what it was like to kiss her and hold her and he was willing to fight for that privilege again.

It made sense.

What didn't make sense was how *he* could feel jealous over a woman he'd only just met. How he felt so... possessive?

He couldn't explain it, but the attraction was there. He liked the way she dealt with JT's stubbornness while leaving the old man his pride. Liked how she doted on her grandfather and the love revealed in her eyes and expression when she looked at him.

That love, that loyalty, attracted him to the nth degree.

Behind him, the kitchen door swished.

"It's not what you think."

Devon lifted his head and found Kelsey staring at him from the opposite side of the massive island. "What do I think?"

"That Neil... Oh, never mind."

"Okay."

"Okay? That's it?"

"You want me to say more?"

She lifted her hand and rubbed her temple. Hard.

"We're not together. It would take a long, *looong* time

for him to rebuild the trust he lost when he-- Neil just stopped by because of the demands of the hospital board."

"Okay."

"Stop saying that! I mean, I get it. Neil is arrogant and prideful, but he's also a good doctor who cares about his patients. A-and people make mistakes and get caught in situations they're not sure how to get out of so sometimes we need to forgive them and move on."

Move on? As in go back with the guy?

Devon narrowed his gaze on her and listened while she rambled on about her ex.

"Do you get what I'm saying?"

He'd tuned out after the forgive them and move on comment but nodded. "You don't owe me an explanation, Kelsey. Your personal life is your own and none of my business."

And he wanted it to stay that way. He didn't want it to be his business because if it was, his jealousy or possessiveness or whatever it was he felt for Kelsey would tip the scale, and he'd need to take the doc to task for using his house call to ingratiate himself to Kelsey.

Emotional blackmail was not okay.

Kelsey crossed her arms over her chest and regarded him with a frank stare.

"Actually... it kind of is."

Devon stared at her for a long moment trying not to read more into her words than she meant, but the thoughts were there in an instant and they didn't go away. "And why is that? Am I missing something?"

The door to the kitchen swung open yet again and JT shuffled into the room, one hand holding his injured side.

Kelsey hurried to her grandfather and took hold of his arm to help steady him.

"JT, you said you'd stay in your recliner. What are you doing?"

"Just saying goodnight. And making sure Devon was settled."

"I am, sir. Do you need any help getting to your room?"

JT looked humbled by the request and nodded.

"I'd be grateful, son."

"I can help you," Kelsey murmured.

"No, I need to talk to Devon. Goodnight, Kelsey."

Kelsey looked taken aback and hurt by JT's use of her given name. Devon had noted JT usually called Kelsey by varying forms of endearments.

Kelsey stood on her tiptoes and carefully kissed her grandfather's cheek

"Of course. Goodnight. You'll wake me if you need anything?"

"I'll be fine with Devon's help."

Devon failed to ignore Kelsey's injured expression then moved to the old man's side, steadied him while they slowly made their way through the house to JT's bedroom suite.

The rooms were a mix of browns and dark woods, with a large sitting area, television and desk.

"She's too fragile, my granddaughter."

Devon helped JT lower himself to the side of his bed and then knelt before the man. "Here. Let me help you get these off," he said as he went to remove JT's shoes. "As to Kelsey… I think she's stronger than you say."

"Strong yes, but fragile all the same. I can see it on

her face. She's beginning to trust a snake not to bite her again even though she's still hurting from the first time around. And it's my fault."

Devon began working on the second shoe and took the opportunity at hand. "Why were we in the alley that night?"

The old man inhaled and shook his head slowly back and forth. "I wasn't thinking clearly."

Devon paused when the shoe laces knotted and stared up at JT. "Are you... missing time? Blacking out? Is that why you hired me to act as your guard? To double as help when you... find yourself out on the streets like that?"

JT closed his eyes and ran a hand roughly over his face, scrubbed hard.

"I hate that you and Kelsey have been hurt in the mess I've caused."

When an answer wasn't an answer—it still was.

Devon returned to work on the shoe and unknotted the strings. "Well, for what it's worth, I think she sees the doc for who he is. But only she can decide who she trusts."

"Maybe so, but the girl's lonely. In my day, a woman her age was usually married, had a family. People in her life to love and to love her."

"She has a family--you."

"Bosh, boy, you know what I'm saying. Kelsey needs a good man in her life. Someone who sees her and not dollar signs whenever he looks at her because of what she stands to inherit one day."

"And you think that's what the doc sees?"

"It's hard to discern anymore. I've spent too much of my life around people trying to get an edge up and make a connection. Maybe I'm more jaded than I should be, but when it comes to Neil, he hurt her badly. Now it's all I see."

"Where're your meds?"

"Kelsey said she put them-- there."

JT pointed to the bedside table and Devon rose, quickly reading the dosing instructions before doling them out, and then retrieved a bottle of water from beside the lamp for him.

Once his meds were down, Devon held out his hands to help JT stand. "You're not going to be comfortable sleeping in your clothes. Where're your pajamas?"

"You don't have to help me, son."

Devon stared at JT and raised an eyebrow high as he waited. Just sitting on the bed while someone else removed his shoes had left JT winded and paler than before. The old man was in pain.

"Top drawer over there."

Devon removed a matching top and pants from the drawer and waited while JT unbuttoned his dress shirt and pulled it from his slacks. Devon hadn't considered he'd be acting as JT's valet, but seeing as how Sheldon had been dismissed and only Kelsey was left home, Devon felt JT was more comfortable getting help from him. The elderly man was concerned. And justifiably so.

Devon helped JT undress by removing the loosened shirt from his arms and getting him into the pajama top. Pulling the pajama pants up over the old man's boxers took a little more doing and when it was done Devon noted JT had a white line around his lips and had lost what little bit of color he'd had left.

"Where to now? You sleeping in bed or do you want to move to the chair?"

"Chair."

Once Devon had JT settled in the recliner, Devon pulled the blanket from the bed and tossed it over JT.

"Thank you, my boy. I feel better already."

Devon grabbed the water bottle and television remote from the bedside table and placed them on one by the recliner, in case JT woke up in the night and needed them. "Get some rest. I'm down the hall but I should be able to hear you if you need something. Or have Kelsey come get me. Otherwise, I'll see you in the morning."

"We still need to talk about Kelsey."

JT's words were slurred. Given his injuries and exhaustion, the meds had kicked in quickly.

"Must make a plan to keep her safe before I go...."

Go? As in, die? "She's safe for now, JT. Just rest."

JT nodded, his eyes closed and feet up in the recliner.

Devon moved to the door and was in the process of pulling it closed when he heard JT roughly sigh.

"Ah, my boy. I knew you'd help me take Kelsey home."

Chapter 21

"He's all settled in."

Kelsey stared out the window above the kitchen sink, aware of the exact moment Devon had joined her in the kitchen. "Thank you."

"Not a problem."

But wasn't it? It was certainly a problem for her.

When she'd walked Neil to the elevator to depart, he insisted she check Devon's employment records. And since she'd wanted so badly to help JT and make sure he had everything he needed for the night, she'd gone down the hall to JT's office to do as Neil requested, using that as an excuse to peek in on JT once Devon walked her grandfather to his room.

But she hadn't just glanced in. No, she'd stayed by the door, out of sight, struck still by the sight of Devon going down on his knees to remove JT's shoes without a hint of hesitation.

And all she could do was watch…and listen.

JT had always been a rare breed. A man who would give the shirt off of his back if someone had need of it.

Her father, too. And both men had taught her it wasn't words but deeds that made a man.

"You seem far away. You okay?"

No, she wasn't. She was confused. But how could she explain that to Devon when she didn't understand it herself? Didn't know who she could trust? "I'm fine."

It's just... the men she knew... Neil and their mutual friends, JT's friends, they were all members of affluent boards and CEOs, men of power and influence who would snap their fingers and someone would come running—

But she'd almost bet her life every single one of them would hesitate or outright refuse before kneeling down to help remove someone's shoes.

And as such none of them drew her curiosity and interest the way Devon did.

How was that possible?

"Look, don't worry about JT asking me to help him. It's no big deal. I'm sure he was embarrassed that he needed help and didn't want to have to ask his granddaughter."

Devon leaned against the counter and watched her, and she managed a nod. "Yeah, you're probably right."

"Where's Bronte?"

"Carlos was on break so he came and got her for a quick walk. They should be back any minute." She plugged the sink and turned on the tap, busying herself as she tried to sort through her thoughts.

"I can take a look at the dishwasher tomorrow if you like."

Kelsey glanced at Devon in surprise. "What?"

"I don't know if I know anything about repairing

things but I'd be happy to give it a shot to try to get it working again. Save a call to a plumber."

Her hair fell forward over her face and she didn't bother trying to hide her smile. Maybe she wasn't the only one who needed to not judge or jump to assumptions. "Who says it's broken?"

"It's not?"

"No. I appreciate the offer to fix it, but it's fine. Dishwashers use a lot of water and... Washing up was something my parents used to do together at the end of the day and doing it, weirdly, helps me unwind. My mother always said that with every dish we had to wash we had something to be thankful for whether it was the food we'd eaten, the company we'd shared it with or the day we'd had, no matter how good or bad it was. Today, I'm grateful JT is home and resting."

She stared down as the bubbles began to expand in the sink, wishing her parents were there to help her with JT. Maybe they'd know what to do. What to say to JT to snap him out of whatever was happening.

"That's a beautiful sentiment."

She went to work on the dishes and forced down the fear trying to take root in her stomach. Things would work out. JT was not crazy. "It *is* a beautiful sentiment, isn't it? After dinner while I did my homework, my mother would wash, my father would dry and they'd talk about the day and their plans for the next. It was a good thing to witness."

"They were missionaries?"

She inhaled and held her breath for a moment before releasing it in a sigh that took none of her worry with it. "Yes. Did JT tell you that or the news reports?"

"I watched a bit of news while in the hospital."

It was hardly news anymore. Gossip TV was more like it.

"You told me to ask about your 'interesting' childhood. Now a good time to get the story?"

She lifted her shoulder in a shrug and slid a glance in his direction. "As good as any, I suppose." She was tired from the last couple of days but also wired thanks to Neil's visit and the anxiety he'd brought. She made short work of the three plates, glasses, and utensils that were used at dinner. "I was born in Africa. I lived there most of the year with my parents in a little village. My father was a doctor as well as a minister. My mother began college thinking she'd study business, but wound up meeting my father and became a nurse instead."

"Sounds like a couple who knew themselves pretty well."

"Yeah, it does, doesn't it? They worked so hard to care for the families who came to them. They were always aware they had a life here to escape to, if needed, but the people there had no escape. In the end, my parents couldn't escape that life, either."

"How so? How did they die? If you don't mind my asking."

Kelsey did mind. It was the last thing she wanted to think about right now with JT's situation pulling her mind in ninety different directions, but for whatever reason she found it easy to talk to Devon. "I had traveled back to the States for the holidays and to spend extra time with JT and Gram. My parents would arrive the week of Christmas and then we'd all fly back to Africa together. On their way out of the village they received word of a group of refugees in need of medical aid but... It was actually a trap set by the local warlord who had grown angry that my parents were helping the people he was trying to dominate. When my parents arrived, he was waiting to ambush them."

"I'm sorry. I can't imagine..."

She accepted his words with a smile. "To be honest, I still can't believe it even though it was a long time ago. I mean, *that's* a story you hear on the news but it's never someone you actually know, much less your parents. And then I think of the people they could have helped through the years since their deaths and how senseless murdering them was... It's hard not to be angry."

"That's understandable. Anyone would be angry. Maybe… I don't know. Maybe think of the legacy they left behind? The people they were able to help will never forget, and maybe they've gone on to help others because of it."

"I suppose. But I'd still like to know why. I mean, it's the same as wanting answers as to why you lost your memory, and why the people who hurt you and JT got away. You protected JT, took a bullet for him. How is that fair?"

"My memory will come back eventually."

She fought her frustration and shook her head. "You're missing the point."

"No, I get it. I just don't agree. People can drive themselves crazy asking why something happened but it doesn't mean we'll ever know the answer. Sometimes we have to accept that it did and move on."

"I'm not good at that. At...letting go." Did he have to make sense? Because man-logic wasn't something she wanted right now.

She wanted answers.

You and everyone else in the world.

"You realize Neil isn't going to do anything to jeopardize the chance of getting back together with you, right? And that includes the fallout of whatever issues JT has? So whatever bluff the doc is using, it's just that. A bluff."

She rinsed the last plate and placed it on the mat to dry. "I can't be sure of that."

"Is that why you're letting him manipulate you?"

"I'm not letting him do anything. I'm simply not rocking the boat any more than it already is. Neil stopping by to check on JT is a hassle and inconvenient but it's better than the alternative. JT should realize that and not make things worse for himself."

"I'm simply saying you hold more power than you realize. Neil's the one dangling on the string between you and the board's demands. Don't allow him to make you think otherwise."

"Is that advice from you--or JT?" She felt compelled to come clean about eavesdropping on Devon and JT. "I heard what JT said to you in his room. I was walking by and... heard you."

Devon didn't look as though he believed her but didn't take her to task for it.

"JT wants to protect you. You can't blame him for that."

"I know. The problem is right now JT needs protection from himself. He can't go to battle with Neil and the hospital board when he's acting the way he is, and until the photos and news articles blow over, JT's every move is being watched by his business associates world-wide."

Devon leaned his hips against the edge of the countertop and seemed to ponder her words.

"You said you listened in."

"I said I heard you," she quickly corrected.

"So you heard me ask if that's why he hired me."

"I did. But he didn't answer you." She smothered a soft groan. "Which means it's a definite possibility."

"Made more complicated by the fact I can't remember the details of our agreement. It's quite the quandary."

Kelsey nodded. "Exactly. I don't know why JT hired you or when, I only know all of this is happening very quickly and very publically. I'm not sure any of us truly know JT's condition because he's smart, smart enough to hide the worst of it until he wants whatever it is to be revealed." Her voice thickened when she thought about all of the possibilities and she had to pause to clear her throat. "JT and Neil both have agendas and I am stuck in the middle."

Devon watched her closely. "Why are you telling me this?"

Why? Telling Devon was such a gamble but it couldn't be helped. She needed to try to gauge whether Devon would be receptive to the bribes or not. "Because like it or not, *you* are now in the middle, too." She lifted her hand and waved it toward the area of the townhouse where JT slept.

"You've protected him not once, but twice now. And minutes ago I watched you... care for him. Whether it's because of the paycheck you receive or the contract you signed or whatever the obligation-- I need to believe that's real."

"You're worried I'll go public about him?"

She hated Devon's expression, the insulted look she'd put on his face with her words. But she had every reason to question his motives and plans, and no reason to trust that he wasn't like all of the others. "People can be bought. Everyone has a price and when the press or the board members who want JT gone figure out what yours might be, they'll come after you and they will be relentless."

"Let them come. I have no reason to do anything they might ask and every reason to be thankful for all that JT's done for me just in the last two days. As to going to the press, I'm sure JT prepared for that with a non-disclosure of some sort."

Devon stared into her eyes and Kelsey had a hard time taking a breath. Drawn to him, she waited, silent.

"Kelsey, I don't remember a lot of things but I think I'm a little old fashioned myself. The thought of taking advantage of JT leaves me angry, okay? My gut tells me that's not who I am."

And there she had it.

The words everyone said at some point to gain her trust… but no one ever meant.

Chapter 22

The following day passed in a blur of playing catch up at the bookstore. Paperwork had to be done, orders made, books shelved, customers handled. Business kept Kelsey running to and fro at a frantic pace, and she was grateful for it because it kept her mind off of JT and Devon.

The city was just as alive at night as it was during the day, and as the evening hours set in, the store had another surge of after-work customers looking for entertainment.

"Need a hand?"

Kelsey startled at the sound of Devon's voice. She stood with the phone to her ear, a pen in her hand, a customer waiting nearby, and one on hold.

"Sorry. I didn't mean to startle you."

Kelsey fought off the tingle of awareness. Devon really was a good-looking man. One presently drawing the attention of several nearby customers both female *and* male.

"I could." The beautiful woman flashed Devon a

seductive smile. "I've been standing here a while and *she's* been too busy to help me, but I'll bet you could help me find what I'm looking for."

Like so many times in her life when she'd come to the city to visit JT and Gram, Kelsey found herself dismissed. Back then it had been by people who would take one look at her average features and non-designer clothes and not connect her last name to JT's. Now that dismissal came from a woman who, if Kelsey wasn't mistaken, ranked a woman's importance by her looks and didn't see Kelsey as competition.

"Uh...Sure."

"Where are the history books? On the founding colonies. It's my h-- uh, friend's birthday and he's into that boring stuff."

Devon glanced at her and Kelsey pointed to the section of the store where those could be found. "Third section from the wall, middle shelf near the floor."

"Impressive," Devon murmured.

The customer drew Devon's attention back to her by placing her designer nails on his arm and snuggling up to his side as she pulled him toward the stacks.

Finally the music playing in Kelsey's ear stopped and she was able to speak with the book dealer who'd had her on hold for ten minutes.

After securing the rare title and answering a question for the customer on hold, she turned and found Devon standing opposite her behind the counter. Once again she startled and he held up his hands as though surrendering.

"Sorry."

"No, it's fine. It's just so noisy in here and I didn't hear you." He looked good. Less pale than he'd been immediately after the head injury and very handsome in the dark pullover and slacks he wore. "I see the clothes arrived."

Devon plucked at the material of his lightweight sweater and gave her a rueful grin.

"They did. Thank you for getting them for me."

"No problem." She leaned her hips against the counter, welcoming the momentary break from chaos, and watched as Devon looked around the store. "Um... Not to be rude but shouldn't you be upstairs with JT? Resting? You are recovering from a head wound, you know."

Devon tilted his head to one side and gave her a look that made Kelsey's insides warm.

"Are you worried about me?"

She flicked her tongue over her lips to wet them and fussed with straightening the counter, gathering up pens and notepads and papers. "You were seriously injured. Of course, I'm worried."

"Kelsey, I'm fine. I haven't had any dizziness today. And to ease your mind further, I didn't leave JT alone."

"You also didn't come down here for a tour or to help strange women find books. Did you need something?"

It wasn't that she minded his company but she wondered at his appearance. When she'd called JT earlier to check on them her grandfather had said a lively card game was taking place.

"Yeah, a change of scenery. Sheldon stopped by and he's sitting with JT until I return."

She shoved a highlighter into a jar with the others. "Did you remember something?"

"No. I came down to familiarize myself with the building and introduce myself to the guards."

Ever the protector. Even injured and recovering Devon took his job seriously. "Oh."

"What about your day? Have you had anymore incidents with the press?"

"Nothing my staff couldn't handle. One of them got a little over zealous with the hunt and mistakenly confronted a woman snapping a photo but it turned out she's a writer working on her NaNoWriMo book simply documenting her location for Instagram."

"NaNo-- what?"

"It's short for National Novel Writing Month, which takes place every year in November. The writer took it all in stride and was thrilled to get free coffee and snacks for the day so she'll probably use the experience in a book at some point."

Devon shook his head but seemed amused by the story.

"I can see why she wanted to photograph her location. I wasn't sure what to expect when you said you had a bookstore but this is amazing, Kelsey."

She couldn't hold back the smile that formed. "Thank you. It is pretty amazing, isn't it? It was a gift from JT after I graduated from business school with a minor in literature."

"That's quite a gift."

"No kidding." She lowered her voice and moved closer. "What makes it even more special is that this building is one of the old ones. The millwork is so ornate and all original. The staircase is a work of art. JT hired wonderful artisans to repair what was needed and to bring the building back to life. Want to hear a funny story?"

He reacted to her smile with one of his own.

"Yeah. But why don't you tell me as you show me this staircase."

He held out a hand indicating for her to lead the way and she did, moving toward the center of the large building. "Well, when JT brought me to see it I was just beside myself. Who wouldn't be? For me, it was a dream come true *and* love at first sight. We stayed for hours and when JT mentioned leaving, I couldn't. I insisted that I wanted to spend the night here. So JT being JT, made some calls, and within an hour a mattress appeared at the door along with sheets and bedding, dinner, a bottle of champagne, dessert, even a reading lamp... I stayed up nearly all night just wondering through the stacks. To this day it's one of my favorite memories."

Just talking about that day made her want to turn back time, back to when JT's health was robust, before he'd taken a downward turn.

"Have you repeated the sleepover since then?"

"Unfortunately, no. But only because the next surprise was learning JT hadn't just purchased a book-store but the entire building. That's how the penthouse came about. He said he couldn't bear the thought of me spending so much time here, so it only made sense to make going home a short elevator ride away."

"Your grandfather sounds like a man who values what he has."

"You're right. He does. I think it's from losing my parents and then Gram. We've only got each other now." The statement reminded her of JT's stay in the hospital, his words about 'going home'. He'd been out of his head then and referred to Yorkton, but she knew death was JT's underlying fear. Not death itself because JT believed in Heaven, but the fear of leaving her alone in the world. And since she had called off her engagement with Neil...

So find someone. Date. Maybe it will set JT's mind at ease. Someone like... Devon?

Chapter 23

"Why books over some other business," Devon asked. "Kelsey… Are you all right?"

"Hmm? Oh, uh, yeah." She waved a hand in front of her face as though waving away the thoughts. "Mmm… Books. That goes back to my childhood as a kid of missionaries. We lived in remote regions eleven months out of the year. I was homeschooled while my parents ministered to the sick. I wasn't very old when I declared that I wanted to help, too, so my mother put me in charge of entertainment."

"Let me guess, reading?"

"But of course," she said, smiling at the memories filling her head. "Since I was born there I knew the various dialects. So I would talk to them and interpret while my father gave them physicals. Then I began reading books to help them learn about the world outside of their village. What began as a way of helping them actually helped me. Especially after my parents

were killed. Books were my escape and coping mecha-
nism when life didn't make sense."

They had reached the staircase. She stopped,
turned, but instead of looking at the beautiful master-
piece leading to the second floor, she noted Devon's
entire focus was on her. She flushed because of it.

"What's your favorite book?"

She laughed at the question. "Book? As in a single
book? No, no, no. That's like choosing a single snowflake
when they're all beautiful and different and unique in
their own way. No, the real question here is what's *your*
favorite book?"

"<u>The Art of War</u>."

Kelsey gasped but Devon looked even more startled
by the revelation. She'd asked the question not expecting
an answer but-- "You remembered that?"

His surprise changed to pleasure and a slow grin
broke across his rugged features. "I did. That's... It's just
weird. You asked the question and the answer was
there."

She grabbed his big hand in hers and gently tugged
him away from the staircase when she saw several
customers eyeing her as though they were going to
approach. Some things were more important right now.
"So maybe we should try some more questions?"

"Go for it."

Devon said the words while lacing his fingers
through hers, distracting her to the point that she missed
the step leading to the rear of the bookstore and
tripped. If not for his grip on her she would've fallen on
her face.

"Careful."

"Yeah. Sorry."

Face blazing with embarrassment, she led him to the quieter area of the store and ignored Amanda's *oooh, gurrrrllll* expression as they passed.

"So, um... Easy stuff first," she said as she loosed her fingers and tried to ignore the fact that she missed the strength and warmth of his large hand. "What's your favorite color?"

"Uh... "

"What?" She stared up at him, waited impatiently for his answer.

"What color are your eyes?"

"My eyes?"

He looked a little sheepish. "It's not a line. They're just an unusual color and... I like it."

Well, that had to be one of the nicest things any guy had ever said to her. "They're blue according to my driver's license but they change color depending on what I wear. Sometimes they look green or gray. Thank you. That's very-- Thanks."

Kelsey's insides fluttered, just like she'd read about in books. For Devon? Can't-remember-if-he's-single Devon?

"You're welcome. You have a driver's license?"

"I do. In college my girlfriends and I wanted to take a road trip to the Florida Keys. You know, drive from New York to Florida along the coast. I was the only one who couldn't drive so... I got it and learned really bad driving habits from three other girls who didn't drive much better than I do. Um... Why is The Art of War your favorite book?"

"Because it can be applied to everything. Not just military strategy but life situations and how to approach them."

"Where do you live?"

His thick dark brows lowered into a V but after a moment he shook his head. "I don't know."

She covered her disappointment with an encouraging smile. "That's okay. We're just doing this for fun. I told you about my road trip. Where have you traveled?"

Devon's mouth parted, the V disappeared and he sucked in a sharp breath.

"Devon?"

"Alaska."

He said it with a measure of awe and excitement. Hope blossomed once again. They were making progress!

"Yeah. I mean, I think I have. It just appeared," he said, lifting a hand and pointing to his head. "Like the book and security information."

"Okay, good. That's great, actually. Are you married?" The words were out of her mouth before she could stop them. She'd be lying if she said she wasn't curious as to the answer but she did *not* mean to ask that question.

"No."

She stared up at him. Waiting for him to add "I don't think so" or some other form of uncertainty but... he didn't.

And, yeah, the thrill of excitement she'd felt at having some success with this impromptu game of questions skyrocketed.

Devon lifted his hand to his face and rubbed hard.

"Ah, who are we kidding? Until my memory returns, I won't know for sure."

But like every rocket that goes up it must eventually come down, and her excitement was no exception.

"Actually, I've been so busy with JT and the bookstore I haven't had time to check, but your employment records would show your marital status. If I can find them in JT's files, we can know for sure. Get your home address and emergency contact information, too."

She'd planned to ask JT about those records tonight after work. She would've last night but once she'd paused outside of JT's room and watched Devon help her grandfather, she hadn't continued her trek because doing so just felt… unnecessary. But if Devon requested the information himself, that would be different. Right?

Devon inhaled and released a soft laugh, the sound of which was a mix of gravel and honey and something entirely masculine. It left her feeling tingly, more than she cared to admit.

"Let's go."

Chapter 24

They moved in unison to the private elevator near her office and Kelsey entered the code and swiped her keycard. The doors opened and as they stepped on Kelsey's heart picked up speed.

A glance at Devon made her think he was just as nervous but the time had come to at least know some basics.

The elevator doors opened at the penthouse, revealing Sheldon in the act of fastening Bronte's leash to her harness.

"Good timing, Ms. Kelsey. I was just about to take her out before bringing her to you."

"Is something wrong?"

"Rita just called. She isn't feeling well. She's okay," the man said. "But, I need to go check on her."

Bronte split her days between the penthouse and the bookstore but this morning the dog had been reluctant to leave JT, who was presently snoring in the recliner, oblivious to their arrival.

"Of course. Go. I'll take care of Bronte," she whispered to Sheldon. "Text me as soon as you check on Rita and let me know how she's feeling."

"Thank you, Ms. Kelsey. I will."

Sheldon walked over to a closet door and retrieved his coat.

"Sheldon... were you aware that JT had hired Devon?"

Sheldon glanced at Devon before meeting her gaze. "No. Mr. Wallingford never mentioned Devon to me. But I didn't know Mr. Wallingford was going out on the streets like that either."

JT might not have shared the inner workings of business dealings with Sheldon over the years but she knew Sheldon was privy to nearly all of JT's life. Surely hiring private security would've fallen under that umbrella seeing as how Sheldon and Devon would be working together at times? "Thank you."

"Is something wrong?"

She pinned a smile to her lips and shook her head. "No. We were just wondering."

Bronte whined and let out a low bark, her signal that she really had to go.

"I'll take Bronte out for her walk," Devon said. "George will let me back up. I don't feel right going into JT's office without him aware. You can look and let me know if you find my file."

Kelsey hesitated a moment, but knew it was probably the best decision. JT's personal office was off limits to visitors. Business meetings held at the penthouse were usually conducted in the den. "Okay. Yeah, I'll see you in a few minutes when you get back. Thank you. For helping with Bronte."

She turned and made her way down the hall to JT's office. She entered the security code and stepped inside.

Kelsey left the door open and moved to JT's desk. Her grandfather was old school and preferred paper over computers, which meant since Devon was a recent hire the file should be close at hand.

The only problem was that JT's desk was littered with files. There were files on potential business deals, charities JT funded, a new business prospectus, a copy of JT's Will--

"What? Why are you here?" she murmured.

JT's Will had been handled long ago so for it to be lying on his desk meant he'd pulled it out for a reason. But why? Because something had happened with his health? Why was it there? What had he changed?

Not what you're looking for.

She tucked it back where it was and kept looking. If JT wanted her to know he'd changed his Will then he'd tell her when he was ready.

There was only one stack of files left to go through when--

Home.

That was all it said on the tab but something told her that the file was much more than the obvious.

She yanked it from beneath the others, flipped open the cover, but instead of details about the penthouse or the building where she stood, JT had drawn a map and listed times and dates with notations beneath.

Number of guards. Descriptions of particular guards. Break times. Average time between patrols?

Oh, Poppy.

The map was detailed and marked the trail to the

farthest point JT had managed to journey underground, the dates he'd gone.

And one name kept appearing over and over again. *Devon.*

Met Devon today.

Devon on duty today.

Devon.

Devon.

Devon.

"Something I can help you find, Kelsey Anne?"

Kelsey startled at the sound of JT's question, looked up to see him standing in the doorway, a pained expression of disappointment marking his bruised face. "I think I found what I was looking for."

JT leaned heavily against the doorframe.

She waved the file like a flag. "You *lied* to me, didn't you?"

"You left me no choice."

"No choice? Seriously? You said you'd confused the story with Devon's name. You said you'd come to your senses."

"I did."

"This is coming to your senses?" She tossed the file onto the desk so hard it created a draft.

"I saw your disbelief and I knew time with Devon was the only way to gain his help. Time for *both* of you to trust me."

She palmed her face with both hands and shoved her long hair back. Unbelievable. And when Neil found out... "You've basically *kidnapped* the man. JT, you have to fix this. You have to tell Devon the truth a-and let Neil run some tests so we can figure out--"

"*We* will do no such thing. You will not say a word."

"This isn't a game, JT. We have to help Devon. He's a person and his family has got to be worried *sick*."

"Why is it so hard for you to believe in me, my dear?"

"Why is it so hard for *you* not to understand? Devon wants answers. *He* is the one who asked me to look at his employee file. He's tired of waiting for his memory to return and wants to know the truth."

"That's unfortunate."

She stared at him, waited for him to elaborate, her heart breaking, bit by bit. She'd need to contact JT's attorney. Get him here immediately. And Neil... Like it or not, she'd have to tell him. Neil would know the best hospitals; have the pull to get JT admitted right away. Before things could get worse.

Worse?

"My dear child, you're going to carry on with my plan, whether or not you believe it to be true."

JT's tone snapped her out of her thoughts. She was, was she? "Why is that?"

"Because to do otherwise means you'll lock me away like the hospital board wants. Would you do that to me, Kelsey?"

JT gave voice to her thoughts and the guilt she felt because of it left her trembling. Not the gentle quiver of nerves but a deep, internal quake that shook her from her deepest core.

Did she have what it took to commit JT? To take away his rights, his freedom? Could she do it knowing he would never, ever look at her the same way again. Was she capable of that?

A noise sounded somewhere else in the house. Seconds later Bronte nudged her way past JT and came bounding to Kelsey, tail wagging and a big goofy dog grin on her face.

Bronte met Kelsey's gaze. The ever-intelligent dog must have sensed her upset because Bronte lost some of her energy and paused to lean her body against Kelsey's legs, one front paw wrapping around Kelsey's calf, as though in a hug.

"This is your moment of truth, my dear. Ah, even better," JT murmured, his gaze fixed on something down the hall only he could see. "Neil and Devon are both here. Just in time for your decision. What's it going to be?"

Thirty minutes later Devon fought his frustration. It didn't take a genius to figure out Kelsey had escaped the penthouse as quickly as possible. But was it because of the doc's arrival, or because of something she'd found in JT's office?

When he and the doc had returned with Bronte, Devon had seen JT standing outside his office door. Kelsey had emerged seconds later, looking pale and flustered.

With Kelsey gone, the doc didn't linger. Neil quickly listened to JT's heart and lungs and performed an assessment then asked Devon a few questions regarding his dizziness and memory. After flashing the penlight into his eyes and making some notes, the elevator doors closed with the doc on the other side. The doc's bedside manner could use some serious work.

Devon battled his impatience to get to Kelsey and wished Sheldon had returned after checking on his wife. "Kelsey left in a hurry earlier."

"That she did. You should go check on her. I'll be fine here, Devon. No worries. I'm in for the night." JT sighed as Devon helped him settle into his recliner. "Get my card for the elevator. There, in the top drawer."

"Thanks. I'll remember to have George get me one tomorrow but he'll need the okay from you."

"Of course."

"JT, you should know I asked Kelsey to go into your office and look for my file. If you're upset with her about that, it's on me, not her. I hope you two didn't have a disagreement because of me."

The old man met Devon's gaze. "You're getting impatient. I understand."

"I want to know."

"Know what, my boy?"

"If I'm… If I have a family. A wife or someone." Devon watched as a smile lifted the old man's face, shifted his mustache and beard.

"I see. It's good that those things are important to you."

"Does that mean you know? Do I have a family?"

JT closed his eyes and settled deeper into his chair, lifting the draped blanket up to his chest. "It'll be fine, my boy. You'll see. You'll both see."

Was that supposed to be an answer? Devon shook his head at JT's odd statement, much like he had the night before, and passed it off as the meds kicking in.

Devon moved through the elegant penthouse and waited impatiently for the elevator to arrive. A minute or so later, the elevator door opened into a semi-dark bookstore. Her office was around the corner and Devon headed in that direction, spotting her through the open door. Computer light lit her face and from where he stood, Devon saw the fear etched in her expression. "Are you going to tell me what's going on?"

Chapter 25

Kelsey gasped, the hand holding the computer mouse flying to her chest as though to keep her heart from jumping out of her chest.

"I didn't hear the elevator. I didn't know anyone was here."

He entered the small office and leaned his shoulder against a tall bookcase overflowing with books. "What's going on, Kelsey? What did you find in JT's office?"

She closed her eyes, shook her head.

"Nothing."

"Kelsey--"

"I'm telling you the truth. I didn't find an employment record or background check on you."

He waited her out, stared her down.

"But there is something you should... There's something I have to tell you, Devon, but I don't..."

"Whatever it is, just say it."

"It's not that simple."

"Why not?"

"Because he's *not* crazy. I need you to believe that. He's just...mixed up."

Devon stepped deeper into the room, closer to Kelsey, not stopping until he rounded the desk and Bronte got up and moved out of the way.

Devon knelt at her feet where she sat in the office chair and took her hand in both of his. "Tell me what's going on."

A gasp of sound left her chest—part sob, part air, all pain. "I don't even know where to start."

"Try the beginning. Why are you so upset? Did the doc come here after he left the penthouse?"

She shook her head. "He can't without a keycard. He has to go out on the street and come in through the door during business hours. H-He texted me wanting me to let him in but I didn't respond. I couldn't. He'd take one look at me and know...."

"Kelsey, what's going on? What are you doing down here?" He glanced at the computer monitor as he'd asked the question and froze when he spotted the missing persons pictures spread across the screen. A glance up at her search words and he felt shock surge through him.

<u>Missing white male NYC</u>

"Would you care to explain... that." When he locked gazes with her again he saw the fear in her eyes. "Sweetheart, what's going on?"

"You said you're a good man. You said you w-wouldn't sue o-or--"

"I won't. Okay? I won't, but spit it out. What is that about?"

"I don't think-- You aren't who JT says you are."

He wasn't sure what to say to that. "So who am I?"

"I don't know. That's why I was searching... To see if someone has reported you missing."

Missing? If he was missing that meant he didn't work for JT. That meant—

Devon shot to his feet and battled a wave of dizziness so strong he felt himself toppling sideways, black spots blinding him.

Kelsey called his name. He heard the office chair clatter as it rolled and banged into something. Felt her arms surround him and press him back against the desk, hold him there, somehow manage to keep them both upright.

"Don't pass out. Oh, please, don't pass out. I've got you. It's okay. I swear it'll be okay but not if you fall and get hurt again. Please don't pass out."

He held onto her like a lifeline, buried his nose in her hair and bear-hugged her until the spots faded.

"Devon?"

A grunt was all he could muster.

"Better now?"

She rubbed his back, slow even strokes he was pretty sure calmed her more than it did him. "Yeah. I think so."

"Sit down in the chair. Please."

At least this time she didn't order him to sit like she did Bronte.

He did as requested, grateful to have the chair's support when faced with the images on her monitor.

"Okay, so... JT's issues... I told you he wasn't thinking clearly th-the night of the mugging, right? "

"Yeah." He waited, willed her to hurry up.

"Well, when they said he was talking out of his head, what they meant was that he… JT thinks you're an elf."

He blinked at her, unable to process her words. "What?"

"Not *really* an elf but someone who works for…."

"Santa? You mean an elf like *that*?"

Kelsey's teeth sank into her lower lip and she nodded, apprehension and fear straining her features.

"I'm sorry! I believed him when he said you were his bodyguard because we've talked about him getting one for a while now—years, actually, but—I promise I'll search until I find out who you are. There's no need to go to the police or the press o-or an attorney. Just give me some time to sort this out."

She dropped to her knees in front of him, mimicking his position from earlier.

"Kelsey, I won't sue you but only if you'll stop bringing it up." He shook his head. An elf? "Do I look like a freaking elf?"

Amusement lit her eyes and she shook her head. "No. I'm so sorry."

Yeah, so was he. Because if his memory would return all of this could be settled. "Is my name Devon York?"

"I-I think so? Well, the Devon part anyway."

"Explain."

"Well…"

She closed her eyes and took a breath and he could see her readying herself up for whatever was about to come next.

"I did find something in JT's office. A file with your name—Devon—in it repeatedly, but it wasn't about employment."

"Let me guess. It was a map to Santa's secret workshop?" She cringed and he gaped. "Seriously?"

She put her hands on his knees and squeezed. "JT said he met you underground in the tunnels but they found you both in an alley after the mugging so maybe that's what he meant? It was late, dark. Maybe in his mind he just thought you were both underground?"

He tried to reconcile the sharp-witted and shrewd elderly man sleeping in the penthouse above their heads with the man Kelsey described. "That's crazy. Kelsey, that's--" He broke off when he focused on her expression, on the hurt the term caused her. "Sorry."

"No. It's completely unbelievable but I'm the one who's sorry, Devon. I don't know what's going on with JT but because of the mugging you've been dragged into it too."

"What are you going to do?"

Her lower lip trembled with the force of her emotions and he loosed his death-grip on the arm of the chair to cradle her jaw in his palm, running his thumb just beneath her lip in an attempt to still it.

"I don't know."

Devon thought of the newspaper articles and photos, the press camped outside her door. The overwhelming amount of love he'd seen her express to JT just in the time he'd known her. None of this was going to be easy, and Kelsey had some very tough decisions in front of her. "I don't know about you but I could use some air. Wanna get out of here and take a walk?"

Kelsey sniffled and nodded. Devon leaned forward and before he could stop himself, he pressed his lips to her forehead, lingering over the feel of her soft skin, the scent of her hair in his nose. "Stop panicking. We'll figure this out."

*A*fter checking in on JT they grabbed their coats and hats, wrapped their faces in scarves, and left the building through an emergency side exit with George's help. Devon held Kelsey's bare hand cradled in his while they dodged icy puddles and ran down the alley to avoid the reporters still lurking outside hoping for a scoop.

Thirty minutes later Devon struggled with an out-of-body feeling as he walked the streets of the city beside Kelsey.

Thanksgiving was only two days away and everywhere he looked there was a mix of fall-colored decorations intertwined with Christmas lights and New Year's Eve advertisements. The sight was as chaotic as his thoughts.

Kelsey didn't talk much during the walk. Every time he glanced down at her it appeared she took in the sights and sounds and smells of the city like it was her last time seeing it this way.

Then it hit him that in reality, it was the last time. Her world had been rocked by her discovery, changed forever because she could no longer deny whatever it was happening with JT.

She'd found the proof—or lack thereof—and now they both needed time to process and formulate a plan. Searching the Missing Persons Reports was a solid start. Going to the police meant exposing JT's failings and deception, and Devon wouldn't do that to them. Not when he knew the impact it would have on them at such a deeply personal level.

He inhaled deeply as he could, appreciated the cold, crisp bite of air after being cooped up in the penthouse apartment and hospital the last several days. Looking up, however, made him feel suffocated by the tall buildings, the lights too bright as they blotted out his view of the sky.

Didn't anyone here want to see the stars?

Devon was glad Kelsey didn't remove her arm from his in the crowd of people. It didn't matter that the sun had set hours earlier. The sidewalks were busy, the streets packed, and everywhere he looked someone or something was coming or going.

They rounded a corner and suddenly he realized why the area was so congested. An ice skating rink had been set up in the middle of some shops and restaurants.

"That looks like a fun distraction."

"Yes, it does."

Kelsey glanced up at him in visible surprise. "You like to ice skate?"

Did he? "Yeah." Like the other answers that appeared out of nowhere, this one did too. "I do. Let's go--ahhh. Sorry. Never mind."

"What? Are you afraid you'll fall and hit your head again? That was my first thought. Especially when you were so dizzy in my office."

"That was because I stood up too fast. No, I just changed my mind." The lame excuse lacked conviction and he knew it.

"Devon, come on. I told you my grandfather thinks you're," she lowered her voice, "an *elf*. I'm not taking another step until you tell me what's going on in that hard head of yours."

He stared down at her upturned face, liking her bluster. "That's not much of a threat. I think I could move you if I so chose."

Kelsey smiled up at him from beneath her long lashes before planting herself in front of him, her hands resting on his wrists where his fingers were tucked into the pockets of his coat for warmth.

Devon felt weak in the knees as he stared down at her. She was such a kind, sweet, beautiful woman. A woman caught up in the mess of her grandfather's making and struggling to cope, much in the way he was struggling with his lack of memory.

More than a little embarrassed, he dipped his head. "I forgot I didn't have any way of paying."

"Oh."

"Yeah. I wasn't thinking."

"That's too bad."

"I know. I shouldn't have said anything."

"No, I mean it's too bad you have such a flimsy excuse because if you're really up for it, I want to skate. Let's go. My treat."

"Kelsey, you've done too much for me as it is."

"Well, now you can do this for me."

The look she shot him was comical and he realized no matter what he said he wasn't going to win. Kelsey had it in her mind that she needed to somehow make up for JT's behavior, and she wasn't going to take no for an answer.

Someone bumped into her and shoved her a bit

closer to him. He couldn't get his hands out of his pockets fast enough to help her, but she steadied herself against his chest.

"Sorry."

"No problem."

Kelsey tilted her head to one side and smiled shyly up at him. Man, she was beautiful. Inside and out.

"We're a pair, aren't we? With all of our apologies? Devon, I *always* want to skate, even though I'm not very good at it. JT and I used to come here every holiday when I was little but...."

"The doc doesn't bring you?" He hurried to change the subject off of her grandfather's aging and the realities of the day. Nothing could be done tonight anyway.

Kelsey grabbed hold of his hand and turned, tugging him toward the pay booth.

"Neil brings me to watch but never skate. He has to protect his hands." She wrinkled her nose. "It's understandable, of course, but it takes the fun out of a lot of events."

He'd say so.

Kelsey rented skates for them both and had even snagged a locker to store their shoes. In short order they headed toward the rink.

The motions of skating came to him like second nature and he pushed ahead of Kelsey before swinging around to face her.

"Hey, you're good at this," she said, hands out to her sides in a bid for balance.

He skated backwards and held out his hands for her to take hold, steadying her. "Yeah, like that," he said, watching her feet. "Nice and even..."

Devon repeatedly glanced behind him to make sure

they weren't about to run into anyone and little by little they made their way around the rink. Kelsey finally started getting the hang of it and found her footing, and when she realized she could trust him to guide her, she lifted her face toward the sky, gripped his arms tighter and laughed. "Having fun?"

Chapter 26

"Yes," Kelsey said, smiling. "I've missed this so much."

Devon pulled her closer and swung around so that he was positioned behind her. He kept them moving, supporting her many wobbles and counterbalancing when needed, grateful the earlier dizziness wasn't a problem.

Her hair blew back and snagged in the scruff on his chin and cheek, tickling, but he didn't mind. They skated in tandem, and he liked how she relaxed against him and let him lead.

They had nearly finished skating their allotted ninety minutes before Kelsey called for a break. He helped her to an exit along the wall and they found a bench a little further down.

"I can't believe how good you are at that."

He shrugged, unable to take credit for something he didn't even know he could do until now. "Seemed to come naturally."

"Hmmm. It is something an *elf* would be good at. Maybe JT's right."

They shared a laugh and Kelsey shrugged. "Go with the flow, right?"

"Right." He liked her attitude. Kelsey faced some tough decisions in the next few days and weeks and he was sure the tears would come at some point but for now, she tried to see the humor in a bad situation. It was one more thing about her that appealed to him.

"I appreciate you keeping me upright out there. I know it was no easy task."

He winked at her. "You do seem to have two left feet."

"You should see me when I try to dance," she said with a laugh. "JT tried to teach me to waltz and gave up. It's hopeless."

"Nothing is ever hopeless. You just haven't found the right partner."

"Mmm. Does that mean you know how to waltz?"

He gave the question a moment. "No. But I think I'd be willing to learn."

Kelsey sent him a shy stare before looking around. She focused on something in the distance.

"So, um, I could really use some hot chocolate. Save our spot?"

Devon nodded, noting the way she had given him a job instead of embarrassing him by handing him money to pay for their drinks.

He watched as she made her way to the back of the line to make sure she made it safely, then began scanning their surroundings while he waited for her to return.

Something about the scenario seemed familiar but

like everything else, there wasn't any one certain thing he could pinpoint and attach to the vague gnawing of a memory.

Just skating.

Snow.

The laughter of people as they circled around...a pond. Near the woods?

There were a couple of bonfires, the smell of wood strong in the air. Laughter.

"Here you go. I hope you like extra whipped cream because they piled it on."

He blinked to awareness, accepting the drink with a murmur of thanks. His hands were numb from the cold now that holding her close to skate didn't warm them, and he welcomed the heat from the cup.

She slid her now gloved hand over his bare one.

"Your hands must be freezing. I didn't think about getting you gloves when I ordered the clothes. I'll find a pair of JT's for you to use when we get back."

Kelsey sat down beside him and cradled her steaming cup.

"Devon… thank you."

"For what?"

"Everything. The walk. Skating." She lowered her voice. "Not losing your mind when you saw me looking up missing persons because of what JT's done. It's… insane. I know that, but—"

""But you love him. Whether he thinks I'm an elf or not, the security stuff seems to fit. I know things I doubt the average guy knows so something about that has to be true. Maybe JT created the file during one of his impaired moments and that's why it doesn't make sense?"

She nodded, her gaze holding his. "I suppose it's possible. JT referred to you as security several times that morning when he was obviously confused. We can hire a private investigator o-or have the police get your finger-prints to see if you're in their system?"

"That sounds like a lot of trouble and expense when my memory could return at any moment and make it unnecessary."

"So you're okay with not knowing?"

That was a tougher question to answer. Yeah, he wanted to know, wanted to remember. But once he knew who he was and had a life to go back to, that life more than likely meant not spending time with Kelsey and that— that didn't sit well. Not anymore. " I've had more memories return every day I've been out of the hospital. And... you are going to need help with JT."

She swallowed hard and tears glistened in her eyes but she blinked rapidly and didn't let them fall.

"I know. He's not going to like what happens next if —*when* I contact people to get him help."

"Maybe if I'm around and he believes I'm whoever, I can persuade him to cooperate."

"You'd do that? I mean, after everything we've put you through however unintentionally, I can't believe you're willing to help. Most people would run away as fast as they can."

She tilted her head to one side and her hair fell over her shoulder in a blond waterfall he wanted to hold. Use to gently pull her close so he could kiss her. "I'm not most people. And unless I'm missing something, you didn't do any of this."

She shivered from the breeze blowing through the rink and, unable to help himself he reached out and cupped her shoulder, drawing her against him to share his heat. Kelsey didn't tense or protest but scooted closer.

He lowered his head so that his cheek rested on her knit hat, his lips near her ear because of the people nearby. "I don't remember a lot of things but I know right from wrong. JT is a good guy. Anyone can see that. If I'd been locked in a dungeon, maybe I'd have a different take on things, but you've both gone above and beyond for me. It doesn't matter if my memories come back tomorrow or in a week, I'll still help you with JT. You have my word."

Kelsey slid her head back along his arm and stared up at him, lifted her gloved hand to his cheek before letting it fall to his chest.

"I wish I knew if you were married."

"I want to kiss you too." He shifted his gaze from her full lips to find her eyes held a wariness he couldn't ignore.

"But we can't. Not until..."

"I know."

She brushed her cheek against his chest. "I won't ever hurt another woman the way I've been hurt. Put someone else through the pain and betrayal... It's not right."

He hugged her closer, tighter, held her by his side and watched the skaters go by because that was all he could do. That, and relish the fact that there were still women in the world who knew right from wrong.

He'd meant what he said. If his memories came back this very moment he'd still help her with JT. She needed someone by her side, someone objective to carry the burden of the days ahead.

When he finished with his drink, Devon took the locker fob from her to retrieve their shoes.

Devon put his on while Kelsey continued to sip her hot chocolate, seemingly lost in thought as she watched the skaters pass. He had a good idea of her thoughts but knew she had to come to terms with JT's future on her own.

After a head-tilting swallow she set her cup aside and began to undo her skates.

"Ahhh."

"What's wrong?"

"Nothing. Just the strap."

"Here, allow me."

He knelt in front of her and lifted her skate-covered foot to his thigh.

"Devon, I can get it. You'll be dizzy when you stand up."

"I know," he said simply. "But let me give it a shot."

Truth be told, he missed the contact they'd shared, and removing her skates gave him another opportunity to touch her. The laces and strap were tangled up pretty good and it took a couple of tries to get the skate loosened enough for her to pull her foot out. When she managed, he kept hold and quickly guided it into the warmth of her boot.

"Thanks."

"You're welcome." He glanced up and paused, taking in the moment so he'd have the memory for the future. Whatever may come.

"Why are you looking at me like that?"

"You've, uh, got some whipped cream on your cheek." He pointed to the area and watched while she hurried to lift her hand and wipe at it. "Yeah, you got it."

She hadn't yet straightened from where she'd tried to untangle the lace and he'd leaned in a bit to undo it, the act putting them in close proximity. So close strands of her long hair caught in the fibers of the knit cap he wore, creating a golden veil over them.

The urge to kiss her was stronger than ever and his gaze lowered to her full lips as he battled the temptation.

"We should get back a-and check on JT."

"Yeah." Right versus wrong, he reminded himself. Until he was one hundred percent sure he wasn't involved with someone else, Kelsey was off-limits. Period.

Devon gripped the bench for support and slowly straightened himself up to combat any dizziness. He waited for her to change out her other skate before taking both sets back to the rental booth. That done, they fell into step beside one another once more, an awkward silence stretching between them with every step they took toward the bookstore.

"Hey, there's the tree. I hadn't seen it yet. It won't be lit until the first week of December but it's still pretty awesome, isn't it? I can't imagine trees that tall."

He'd seen bigger.

A wave washed over him. Awareness.

Another memory?

He wasn't sure what it was, only that he felt it and he knew for a fact he'd seen larger trees than the one before him.

"Devon?"

The truth was there but out of reach. If only he

could-- Why couldn't he remember? "I remembered something else."

"Something else? Tell me."

"It's hard to explain but I've had flashes all day. Images that just...appear when things are mentioned. Like the tree."

She urged him off to one side and he followed her direction without question, letting her lead him out of the flow of pedestrians and into a nook created by a building's display window and support wall.

Her expression looked so earnest, so anxious, he inhaled and said, "Nothing personal like my favorite book or confirmation of my marital status," he clarified, enjoying the way she glanced at him shyly from beneath her long lashes. "But things like the fact I've seen bigger trees."

He stared into her beautiful eyes, the gray-green orbs clouded with worry and excitement both. The light from the store's interior cast shadows and highlights over her face and he studied every one, memorizing them.

"Why didn't you say something?"

"They're not actual memories of people or information that's useful."

"But it's progress."

"Yeah, I guess it is."

"So these images. What are they of?"

"Snow. And lots of it. I've seen my feet in snowshoes. And I've remembered skating around a pond, too, near woods. Trees bigger than that one," he said, lifting his hand to indicate the one in Rockefeller Center."

She leaned against his chest and he welcomed her warmth. Bits of snow floated in the air and tucked where they were, it was as though they were in their own little snow globe.

Once more his mind opened and an image formed. "Hands," he murmured. "Wrapped around a snow globe. It had this—This ethereal glow. There were people around me, bundled up for the cold, beneath the moon. Some sort of ceremony."

Kelsey placed her hand on his chest and he grasped her fingers in his, holding them in place for the sole reason that it gave him a sense of security and more pleasure than he'd thought possible. But that's how it was with her. Simple touches, shared gazes, smiles. That's all it took to draw him in, make him wish for more.

"Okay. So deep snow and large pine trees? So you think you might be *from* Alaska, like you mentioned before? Or maybe Canada?"

He shrugged, unable to answer yes or no with any confidence. "I remember seeing a small village. I guess it's a possibility."

"Do you remember anything else?"

He shook his head, searching his mind while he stared into her eyes....

Then remembered a thought he'd had while still in the hospital about women and their dogs. His gut tightened with unease.

Did the thought reference a woman in his life? Girlfriend? A wife?

If only he could remember....

Chapter 27

Devon finished dressing the next morning and walked over to the large windows. He'd come awfully close to kissing Kelsey on several occasions last night and a part of him regretted that he hadn't followed through while he'd had the chance.

But this morning...

The dream he'd had during the late night hours came back to him and he ran a hand over his face.

Who was the woman in his dreams?

Also blond, he'd watched her walk ahead of him out of a building and into snow falling heavily from above. She'd turned and said something to him but he couldn't make out the words. She'd been angry with him and upset. Her expressions indicated as much. But who was she to him?

Devon looked down at his shoes and frowned. That was different, too. The dream flashed in his mind's eye and he saw himself wearing camo pants and black lace up boots, the kind worn by the military.

So if that was the case, he would be listed in a database somewhere, right?

Someone knew if he was married.

Maybe Kelsey's idea of going to the police and having them trace his fingerprints was a good one. At least then he'd know, one way or the other. But he'd cost JT enough and hated the thought of exposing JT should the press discover it, and given the scrutiny JT was under, being discovered was a very real possibility.

His head began to pound. The confines of the room closed in on him. He had to get out of there before he possibly wound up sharing a padded room with JT.

Devon quickly straightened his bedroom before walking toward the door. Rita worked for JT and Kelsey, not him, and he didn't want to add to her workload.

"There you are, my boy. I've been waiting for you," JT said as Devon entered the living room.

"Morning."

"Good morning. Are you up for an adventure?"

An adventure? Devon stared at the man. "What kind of an adventure? You know you have to take it easy."

"I know, I know. That's where you come in," the elderly man said, his head bobbing up and down. "I might not be up to lugging around boxes but from the look of you, I'd say you'll do fine."

Devon shrugged. He didn't care what JT needed help with so long as it kept him from thinking about kissing Kelsey. "What do you have in mind?"

JT scooted to the edge of the recliner and released a soft grunt as he slowly stood.

"Come, my boy. You'll see."

Devon followed JT onto the elevator, noting the old man looked to be feeling better today. He wasn't as pale and while JT had still held his ribs when rising from the recliner, he'd lowered his hand once he was upright.

The elevator doors opened and Devon noted they were in the lower basement level of the building. Where was still a mystery, but JT pulled a keycard from his pocket and shuffled off.

"Kelsey and I haven't done this in a long, long while," JT said, his voice echoing off the concrete walls. "But I think this is the year to bring back the tradition."

Devon didn't pretend to understand but stood patiently waiting while JT entered what appeared to be a storage room, a fact confirmed once the man switched on the lights.

There were boxes stacked everywhere, some old furniture, and a few toys that must have belonged to Kelsey as a child. "Nice bike."

He pictured the girl he'd seen depicted in the photos in the penthouse riding the bright purple bike with it's fancy streamers coming out of the handlebars and the basket on the front, and smiled.

"Yes. She loved riding it in the park. She outgrew it and went on to other things but I couldn't part with it. Not after losing her mama," JT murmured, his tone a bit thick. "She had one very similar to it back in the day. Now let me see... Where did they put it?"

Devon continued scanning the various boxes and items along the path JT took through the maze. He looked up after JT had turned a corner and a feeling of deja-vu swept over him. Had he been here before? Or was it just that it seemed familiar somehow?

The walls were a mixture of concrete supports and brick. Old brick from the look of it.

A loud ripping sound filled the air and he turned to find the source.

"Here, my boy. Come help me, please."

Devon put his feet in motion and found JT rummaging around inside of a dust-coated box. "What's that?"

"What we're doing today to surprise Kelsey."

A surprise? He peered over the old man's shoulder and saw carefully packed Christmas ornaments inside.

"My Celia picked these out herself along with Annabelle and, later, Kelsey. Celia said no amount of money or hired help could do what a family should do together."

"This is Kelsey's surprise?"

"Yes. I can't think of a better one," JT murmured. "Think you can carry these to the elevator for me? You can't drop them, son. My heart would break."

"I'll be extra careful." Devon grabbed hold of the first box and lifted it with ease. "I'll take this out and be right back for the others."

"Good, good. The tree should be arriving any moment. I've already made the call."

Devon left JT with the many boxes and traversed the path to the elevator before he returned for several more loads.

He made the mistake of trying to carry two large boxes stacked on top of one another and even though they were light, seeing over them was an issue. Rather than chancing running into something or worse, dropping one of the boxes and breaking JT's heart, Devon left one of the boxes behind to carry the other safely out.

The stack by the elevator doors grew in size and

Devon returned one last time to find the older man sitting on a crate marked "art". "You okay?" When JT realized Devon was there, the elderly man sniffled and straightened.

JT nodded and wiped a hand under his nose.

"Fine, fine. Just reminiscing. Look here at my girls."

Devon moved closer and stared at the picture JT indicated.

"Kelsey's mother, Annabelle, Kelsey, and my Celia." JT tapped the photo several times with his finger. "I believe Kelsey is now about her mama's age in this photo."

"They're beautiful," Devon stated. Kelsey favored her mother and grandmother. "You're a blessed man."

JT looked up at Devon, his expression softening.

"Most people always said I was lucky. I'm glad you know the difference."

Devon indicated the box where the photo had been found. "You want to take that upstairs?"

"Yes. It shouldn't be down here. When I mourned my Celia I had a company come in and clean things up for Kelsey and me. Neither one of us was in any condition to handle it ourselves. Everywhere we looked there were reminders. These were supposed to have been stored in a bedroom in the penthouse, but must have been brought down by mistake."

Devon watched as the old man placed the photo back into the box and reverently closed the flaps. When JT finished, Devon picked it up and followed the man back through the storage room and into the area outside of the elevator.

JT looked pale once again and seemed to be in pain, no doubt from bustling around in the basement. "Stay here. I left one of the boxes inside. I'll grab it and be right out."

Devon hurried back inside but when he returned to the area where he thought he'd left it, he didn't see the box. He found his way to where all of the boxes had originated and retraced his steps, realizing he'd taken a wrong turn somewhere in the large room stacked in memories.

He walked a different way, moving toward the back of the room and there it was, setting off-kilter atop another. He lifted the box and started to turn when he noticed an arch in the old brick wall with a patterned medallion gracing the center. He stared at it, unable to move for a long moment.

The brick and stone and concrete, old, old brick... That medallion.

He set the box aside once more and moved closer to the wall, visually following the line to where it went behind yet another tall stack of boxes.

He placed one hand on the wall, one on the boxes, and leaned in to see if he could see between the two. The boxes shifted easily.

Frowning, he lifted one of them and shook it gently.

Empty?

Devon replaced the box and carefully bent to see if he could shift the entire stack. No resistance. Either whatever was packed inside was light as a feather or all of the boxes were empty, which is what he suspected. Taped closed and stacked as if they were full.... Why go to the trouble?

The overhead lights provided just enough illumination to allow him to see a small door behind the boxes.

Was it a coincidence it was hidden behind the boxes, or on purpose?

"Devon?" JT called.

"Yeah. Sorry, JT. I set the box down and it took me a minute to find it." The news reports from his hospital stay replayed in his head along with Kelsey's description of JT's behavior last night...

Was *this* how JT got into the tunnels?

"Find something?" JT asked from behind Devon.

Devon turned and nodded, deciding to ask the source. "Yeah. I saw this and had to take a closer look. Where does the door go?"

JT's bushy eyebrows lowered over his nose in a white V before he smiled.

"I'll tell you what I told Kelsey as a child. It's just a door--but it leads to a land not so far away. Now, quit dawdling. We've got lots of work to do."

"Oh, boy. Bad news," Amanda muttered from where she sat.

"What's that?" Kelsey had her back to Amanda and was going over the receipts and paperwork from yesterday's sales. Amanda had a tendency to release quite a few huffs and sighs and mutters as she read her favorite tabloid every morning once the opening assignments were completed. Kelsey tuned out whenever possible.

She didn't care who was reportedly dating whom, where aliens had landed, or what diet some actress was on who didn't need to be dieting in the first place.

"Um... Kels?" Amanda murmured. "You wanna 'fess up?"

"What?" She was having a hard enough time concentrating on what she was doing without Amanda's chatter.

"When--better yet who--is Tall, Dark and Handsome? Wait, is *this* the guy who--"

Something slammed down on the checkout counter near her and Kelsey jumped, startled by the sudden bang. Amanda let out a small shriek as well and both of them turned to glare at a red-faced Neil.

"What is this?"

Kelsey's heart had yet to slow from being so startled and in the face of his anger she struggled to control her own instinctive response. "What are you talking about? And how did you get in? We aren't open yet."

"I walked in with one of your employees."

"Someone needs to get fired," Amanda said under her breath.

"Kelsey, what is this?"

Chapter 28

Kelsey blinked at Neil's overbearing tone and attitude. "I have no idea what you're talking about."

Amanda cleared her throat and rattled the papers in her hands. Kelsey looked from Amanda to Neil and then down, realizing that's what he'd slammed down in his anger. A knot formed in her stomach and she felt like the kid who'd been called out in class for passing notes. "What now?"

Neil shoved the tabloid clenched in the fist toward her and from all appearances it took herculean effort to release his grip. She had to run her hand over the pages to smooth them but when she saw the photos-- *Oh. Boy.*

The pictures were somewhat grainy because they'd been taken at night but her face was very clear in each and every one. Scattered across one entire page were images of her and Devon walking arm and arm. Another of them skating with Devon cradling her from behind while she looked up at him, smiling. Two more, both of them taken when they were face-to-face, nearly nose-to-nose, and looking very much like they were about to kiss.

From Doc to Jock! Has the Billionaire Heiress finally found love?

"Explain."

She stared at the photos in shock. If she hadn't already hated the press this was reason number five-billion-*and-one.*

She didn't want to be in their paper but her wishes didn't matter. And while she'd thought she and Devon had managed to elude the photographers and press lying in wait, obviously they hadn't. "We went for a walk."

"That looks like way more than a walk."

"Um, as much as I hate to interrupt," Amanda murmured. "There are people waiting outside the door and it's time to open. You two might want to take this somewhere private or else risk more of...*that.*"

Kelsey had to bite her tongue to keep from saying something she shouldn't and set aside her task to leave the counter. "Come on. We'll finish this upstairs. Since you're here you can check on JT and you won't have to come back tonight."

There. Let Neil think about that before using that tone with her again.

She stalked ahead of Neil into the back of the large store and hit the elevator button with way more force than necessary. Then twice more when the doors didn't immediately open.

JT wasn't in any shape to be doing anything so why was the private elevator busy?

"He's a total stranger," Neil muttered. "Have you forgotten that?"

Neil stood behind her much like Devon had last night but Neil's hot breath blowing on her ear didn't send chills down her spine the way Devon's did. "I don't owe you an explanation. The fact I'm going upstairs to listen to you rant at me is a courtesy, Neil. Not an obligation."

It was a struggle to keep her voice to a whisper but she managed. Somehow.

"He could be married. Gay. You have no idea."

"He is definitely not gay."

Neil sucked in a sharp breath, his body nearly vibrating with his anger.

"Neil, we aren't together anymore."

"You know I want to change that. I've made that abundantly clear."

"Yes, you have. You've also used JT's health and the hospital board's *request* to push yourself back into my life."

"I got JT released when he should have been in a psych ward."

"So you could come to our home every night. You don't even call or text first. You just show up."

"Is being in my presence such a bother to you?"

She closed her eyes and fought her frustration. Where was the freaking elevator? "You're deliberately missing my point. Just like your preferences have always ranked above mine."

"Fine. Okay, I get it. I can do better."

"I know you can. But do you want to?" She glanced around them to make sure no one was within hearing distance.

"Of course. But I don't like you not giving me the time of day only to wake up to pictures like those."

"This entire argument is pointless. There's nothing between Devon and me-- just like there is nothing between you and I."

"There is still an *us*, Kelsey. And whether you see it or not, Devon is a man while you're a *very wealthy* woman."

She stiffened from her toes to the very top of her head. She didn't ever want someone to consider her vain or stuck on herself but to hear Neil say the only reason Devon--or any man for that matter--would want her was for her grandfather's money... That *hurt*.

His words brought back all of the feelings of insecurity and doubt and animosity she'd felt because of the kids at school and most of the people in her life. Money had a way of attracting people like that, those who wanted to be near solely for their own benefit. "I'm doing okay. My *grandfather* is wealthy."

"Now who's deliberately missing the point? Kelsey, I'm trying to protect you. Why can't you see that?"

The elevator seemed to be stuck on the penthouse floor. At least that's what it looked like through the glaze of angry tears covering her eyes. "I think you would say just about anything to keep me from getting to know someone else. S-so I go back to you."

Neil placed his hand on her shoulder and gently squeezed. She wanted to avoid the contact but couldn't without making a scene and possibly attracting attention from the customers now within sight of them. The last thing she needed was a photo of her and Neil on *tomorrow's* cover detailing some sordid argument.

"Fine. There's some truth to that statement because of how I feel for you. I admit it, okay? But that's not why I'm concerned. JT brought a total stranger into your home and after how many days, you and he are on the front page? That's no accident. JT has always tried to protect you but his mind is slipping, Kelsey. We know that for a fact. Now this Devon person appears out of nowhere and JT invites him to live with you?"

She shouldn't allow Neil's jealousy and skepticism to cloud her impression of Devon but, like it or not, he *was* getting to her. Neil stated all of these issues thinking JT had hired Devon as a bodyguard, but if Neil found out that JT had lied about who Devon was... Could this be some sort of con? A schedule?

"Kelsey, you have to admit it's questionable. There's got to be more to this guy. What if... Just hear me out. What if Devon saw an opportunity? JT was inordinately confused that night. Who knows if it's happened before. Maybe in Devon's presence? And Devon has been waiting for an opportunity by planning the mugging to take advantage?"

Kelsey hugged her arms around her front and shifted to face him, shrugging off Neil's hand in the process. "JT is fine." But he wasn't. And Devon knew that for a fact because she'd *told* him. Confirmed that JT was having cognitive issues. But what if Devon *had* already known? What if the memory loss *was* an act? Was it possible?

She struggled to keep it together in front of Neil. She needed time to sort through this. Time to dig into Devon's history. He'd deflected her offer to go to the police and have them check his fingerprints citing exposure to JT's issues, but she could have it done without his knowing.

"I know you don't want to hear this, especially not from me. But you're overlooking the fact that it could have all been a set up. Kelsey, think about it. What are the odds that JT would've been mugged with a body-guard at his side? The fact that no one has reported Devon missing or gone to the police or hospital in search of him? And, yes, I've checked. No one has. Don't you believe all of that is a little suspect?"

Neil's words cemented fear into her rampant thoughts. Was Devon devious enough to have set all of this up? Was he pretending to have amnesia?

Finally the elevator began to move. She watched as the numbers lowered and the lift arrived with a *ding*. "I don't want to talk about this anymore."

"Using his position as JT's bodyguard is a strategic way of getting close to the one person who stands to inherit a fortune, when the time comes. And by the look of those photos, it hasn't taken him long at all, has it?"

"Nothing happened." The scrape on Devon's head-- was it really a gunshot wound? Had Devon hired the men who'd mugged JT just so he could "rescue" her obviously confused grandfather and endear himself?

"That's what I said, too, but you didn't believe me, Kelsey. People like JT are targets. That makes you a target. You know that. You can't be that naïve."

Was that it? Was that what was really going on?

Neil stepped onto the elevator with her and she fought the urge to step right back off. She needed a moment to herself where she could process everything. Figure out what was real, what were doubts instilled by Neil's accusations, and what came from her own insecu-rities and trust issues. And how all of that played into her relationship with Devon.

She stayed on one side of the elevator, her gaze fixed on the numbers displayed, while Neil leaned against the wall next to her. She could feel him watching her, and she remembered how wonderful it had once felt to be on the receiving end of such handsome attention from him.

But, like her mother had always said, it was what was on the inside of a person that counted. Looks faded, but character didn't.

But what if Neil was right about Devon? Did Neil recognize that—that *deceit*—in Devon because Neil was aware of it inside himself?

The doors opened once more and Kelsey hurried off only to stop in her tracks.

"Kelsey, you're back early." JT frowned at her from his recliner when he saw the look on her face. "Now before you get upset, my dear, I have my reasons."

The three men currently driving her insane stared at her while waiting for her reaction, and all she could do was stare at the Christmas tree and the boxes of painful memories scattered across the floor. No wonder the elevator had been busy.

"Kelsey," Neil murmured, his tone soft and filled with concern. "Sweetheart, are you all right?"

She shook her head, speechless that JT would do such a thing without consulting her first. It was yet another example of his behavior change. Another example of his cognitive level because *her* JT would never have done this. Never have hurt her like this.

Neil took hold of her elbow.

"Kelsey, come on. Come with me."

She stared across the room toward the tree and JT, too hurt to consider Neil's motives, or Devon's, and allowed herself to be pulled back into the elevator.

"Kelsey... My dear, come back. Let me explain."

JT called her name several more times but she

ignored him. Her grandfather knew how hard the holidays were for her. That JT would be so cruel as to disregard her sentiments and do all of that without even consulting her…

Her gaze locked with JT's as the elevator doors closed. In the silence that followed she could hear her pulse pumping in her ears.

"Where's your coat?"

She turned to stare at Neil and had to concentrate to remember if she'd carried one with her downstairs to the bookstore to have if needed or if she'd left it in the penthouse. Kelsey was so scattered by what had just happened, she shook her head. "I don't know."

Neil shrugged out of his long coat and wrapped it around her, tugging her close in the process. She closed her eyes and leaned against him, let him hold her because as badly as she wanted to be strong and firm and stand on her own two feet, that was how badly she needed to be held right now.

Neil might have done her wrong in the past, but right now he was the enemy she knew.

Chapter 29

Later that evening Kelsey spotted Devon the moment the elevator doors parted. He lifted his head from his task and stilled, watching her measured steps. "I thought you'd be finished with that by now."

Bronte ran to Kelsey and rubbed her big, fluffy body against Kelsey's legs. Kelsey petted her and greeted the dog with a kiss on top of her pointy Doodle head.

"JT called a halt to things when you left. He wanted to talk to you before we did anything else."

Kelsey shifted her gaze to the string of lights in his hands and those twinkling on the tree branches. "If that's the case, why are you doing that?"

"Because it means so much to your grandfather."

She heard the censure in Devon's tone and she didn't like it. She crossed her arms over her front as she walked around the couch to sit down. "Since when? JT doesn't like decorating or celebrating anymore than I do. It's not our thing. Hasn't been for years."

"Maybe he hasn't in the past but this year is different."

Yeah, this year was definitely different. "Why is that?"

Devon refocused on lighting the limbs and she caught herself staring at his strong profile and comparing him to Neil.

Neil had hailed a taxi and swept her away from the building earlier. They'd gone back to his apartment and fixed a simple lunch together and talked. He'd asked her to attend the hospital gala together, like they had the previous year, and she'd been so upset over JT and the stupid tree and the possibility that Devon was a con artist faking his memory loss, that she'd agreed to the invitation.

"You'll have to ask JT that. But I do know going down there today and getting all of this stuff from storage wasn't easy for him."

He lifted a finger and pointed to a box near the couch.

"Especially when he found that one."

More than a little intrigued by Devon's comment, Kelsey shifted on the couch, shoved a needy Bronte out of the way, and opened the flaps. She caught her breath and had to swallow hard to rid herself of the lump that formed in her throat.

"JT said they must have been put into storage by accident."

She nodded, knowing it was true. The penthouse had no shortage of space and the room located beside JT's office had become storage for items too susceptible to ruin. Items like photos and home movies, her grandmother's wedding gown.

While Devon worked on the lights, she picked through the photos and cards. Pictures of her mother and Gram, birthdays and holidays long gone. One after another she stepped back in time to when her parents and grandmother were alive and it slowly dawned on her why JT had chosen this year to resurrect the tradition.

He wanted at least one last Christmas to remember. That had to be it. JT's strange behavior, his injuries. His health and age. He was afraid. Her grandfather who didn't fear anything, was afraid.

Not of dying, but of her not having *this* to hold on to. To get her through the years to come if this was—

What? His last year?

When she thought of the years they'd wasted. Years they could have gone on and continued to decorate and enjoy the holidays together...

She rubbed her temple. Then she realized that with all of the talking she and Neil had done earlier, not once had Neil mentioned specifics about JT's health. Nor had he shared with her the results of the many scans and tests he'd run. Why was that?

The weight of her thoughts seemed to pull her deeper into the couch cushions as reality sank in. Neil had simply released JT--with the caveat that Neil was allowed to check on JT every day.

Which meant either JT was okay--or he really, really wasn't.

"What has JT told you about his health?"

"Nothing. The only thing I know is what you've told me."

She studied Devon for a while as he lit the tree

branch by branch, watched for any signs that indicated he attempted to mislead her as Neil insinuated.

Devon paused in his work and met her gaze.

"If you have something to ask me, ask. Staring a hole into me isn't going to give you whatever you're looking for."

She inhaled and pulled a pillow from the couch across her lap to hug. "Has your memory returned?"

His expression revealed his surprise. But good acting could do that as well.

"I would've told you if it had."

"But you did actually lose your memory?"

Devon's gaze narrowed and he shoved the strand of lights into the tree in a clump. He held her gaze while he moved toward her, crouching down in front of her.

"You don't believe that's true?"

"I don't know what to believe anymore."

"Kelsey, where is this coming from?"

She looked away from him, unable to stand the hint of hurt she saw in his gaze, only to meet them again.

"I saw the photos of us. Is that what this is about?"

She watched as he slowly shifted from his position on the floor to the couch beside her, his arm falling behind her along the back. He smelled good, like the woodsy soap kept as one of the options for guests. "No. Well, yes, if I'm honest I guess it's part of it but... not all."

"Care to explain?"

How could she? If he was trying to pull a con over on JT and her it wasn't as though Devon would confess to it. She lifted her hand and covered her eyes, rubbed, trying to release some of the tension. "It's been a long day. A long few days and Thanksgiving is here. Black Friday."

She didn't sound convincing but how could she say more than she already had? Accuse him of something <u>worse</u> than faking memory loss? Only time would tell and until then she had to balance both possibilities and the potential fallout.

"You are under a lot of pressure but if you're questioning me faking my amnesia and trying to fool you, I should leave."

It would be best, Kelsey thought, but at least here, Sheldon and Rita could keep an eye on him, and in their loyalty report any strangeness. As to Devon using his stay as an opportunity to get close to her... What was the saying? Keep your friends close and enemies closer? "Where would you go?"

"I'll figure something out. JT paid me in cash since I don't remember where my bank is or if my wallet was stolen that night. I'll be fine. I'd rather go to a hotel than stay knowing you have doubts about me."

When Kelsey looked into his eyes she didn't have doubts. Devon seemed sincere and kind and caring. Protective.

And if that wasn't enough, she'd promised JT this time with him. It had only been a matter of days since the mugging and if Devon was telling the truth, the flashes of memories were happening more and more frequently. That meant the "week or so" timeline Neil had quoted Devon in the hospital was coming to an end and would either prove true--or Devon would have to subject himself to more tests and procedures to figure out why his full memory hadn't returned. Would a con artist take things that far? To such extremes as to endure poking and prodding of invasive tests?

She needed a plan. To establish boundaries. She

would keep her guard up. "I want you to stay. Ignore me. My mind is just all over the place at the moment and I'm worried about JT. Surely you can understand that?"

He sucked in a deep breath and leaned away from her. "What?"

"This isn't entirely about JT, is it? What did the doc say about you and me and those photos?"

"You saw them?"

"They made the evening news along with the ongoing mystery of JT's adventures."

She shook her head and groaned. "Great."

"Kelsey…."

"The pictures aren't an issue."

"Obviously they are."

He leaned forward on the couch and braced his elbows on his legs, hands clasped in front of him as he watched her.

"Care to let me take a guess?"

"Devon--"

"We had a nice time last night and those photos made it look pretty cozy. I'm guessing the doc didn't like that."

"He...didn't." Understatement of the year.

"So he probably implied I'm trying to romance you? Get close to the heiress?"

She didn't confirm or deny but she really didn't think it was necessary. Especially when Devon muttered something under his breath.

"Devon, I don't want to believe that about you, about anyone, but I'd be... irresponsibly naïve if I didn't consider the possibility. Please don't take offense."

But he had. She could read it in his stare, the tension in his body.

"What do you want to do about the tree? Do you want me to stop until you can talk to JT?"

Wait. What? That was it? End of conversation?

She opened her mouth to try to reopen the subject of *them* and their relationship--whatever it was--only to close it because it was obvious to her that Devon had shut himself off. Shut her out. Set a boundary. Wasn't that what she wanted?

Time. Everything is revealed in time. Let it be.

She pulled her gaze away from his profile to stare at the twinkling lights, thinking of all the reasons JT might have for wanting to celebrate. "JT wants to do this?"

"It certainly wasn't my idea."

"Well, then... I guess we'd better light up the tree and have it ready to decorate after we eat Thanksgiving dinner tomorrow."

*D*evon stared at JT and tried to comprehend why a man JT's age would consider doing such a crazy thing. "You want to go *shopping*?"

Thanksgiving Day had come and gone, thick with tension. Devon understood why Kelsey's ex discredited him, but it didn't mean he was okay with it.

Kelsey wasn't much better. Quiet, withdrawn.

After strained conversation and a meal he didn't really taste, they'd made their way to the tree, where he, Kelsey and Neil subjected themselves to JT's advising as to where to place each piece. Once they'd finished with the official lighting of the tree, she'd excused herself immediately.

"Today's the day people shop. The TV said so."

"JT, you're not exactly 'people'. And you're injured."

"Bah, my ribs aren't nearly as sore as they were. Besides, you'll be there to help me. Oh, that reminds me. I'm accepting the invitation to the hospital gala. What size tux do you wear so my assistant can get you one?"

Devon raked his hands over his face, remembering Kelsey's comment about him having his hands full trying to guard JT. But was he JT's guard? Until his memory returned, the simple answer was yes. "You want to go to a gala?"

"Come on, my boy. Keep up! I'm twice your age. Aren't you tired of sitting here listening to me snore? Where's your Christmas spirit?'

Christmas spirit? He thought of the logistics of trying to protect JT in the crowds outside and cringed. "JT, you're a billionaire. Call someone. When you tell your assistant to get me a tux also tell them what you want and have it delivered. Isn't that typically the way billionaires do things?"

"Sometimes but not this year. I want to pick things out myself. Take it to the streets and shelters and see their faces when the people get it."

Streets and shelters? "JT, going out on the streets is how you got us both injured. Do you remember that?"

"Your memories will come back. They already are somewhat, aren't they?"

"Not the point."

"Well suck it up, son. We're going Christmas shopping."

An hour later, Devon murmured his appreciation to

the toy store manager and escorted JT through the crowd and into a storage area. If the store wouldn't accommodate a billionaire, they took JT's business elsewhere.

"Why are we in here? The toys are out there."

"This is a compromise. Everything displayed out there is also back here. You can do your shopping here and I can do a better job at keeping you safe."

JT narrowed his gaze and grumbled under his breath but Devon didn't back down. Finally JT focused on the floor-to-ceiling toys waiting to be taken out front and began wandering through the organized aisles followed by a store employee and a scanning gun.

An hour passed. Then two. And after JT had bought out most of the store's reserve, he had his assistant arrange for deliveries to the local shelters as well as hire a box truck.

"You're renting a truck? You want to fill me in on the plan?"

"You and I are delivering the truckload ourselves. The rest can be taken to the shelters."

"JT, you're going to start a riot."

"Nonsense, my boy. We're just going to have some fun."

A riot didn't sound like fun. "Well, the toys are nice but don't you think it's a little impractical? Toys aren't going to keep anyone warm or fed."

The old man's gaze took on an amused glint.

"Good thing we're just getting started then, isn't it?" JT clapped Devon on the shoulder. "Come on, boy, you're slowing me down!"

———————————

Chapter 30

———————————

Ten hours later Devon decided the day's biggest battle had been getting the store managers to <u>stop</u> bringing out new items for JT to purchase. Before it was all over, the city's shelters were stocked with food, blankets, and sleeping bags, and JT had even hired a mobile street vendor to do nothing but cook and serve food to the homeless while Devon and JT emptied the truckload of items JT wanted to hand deliver.

JT was visibly exhausted and in pain by the end of the day but anyone could also see the pleasure on the old man's face. JT had broken down more than once listening to the stories of those on the streets, and Devon would be lying if he said a few of them hadn't choked him up as well.

Once home, JT had said he was too tired for dinner and Devon followed the elderly man to his room in case he needed help with his shoes. JT waved him off, declaring himself fit enough to get himself to bed.

"You did an amazing thing today, JT. I wasn't too

thrilled by the idea, but I'm glad you let me be part of it."

JT unbuttoned his sleeve cuffs.

"It was fun, wasn't it? But I'm sure you've done charitable work before. You were a natural."

Devon couldn't remember if he had or not but in any case it would be a part of his future. "Call if you need anything."

"Night, son."

Devon went to the kitchen in search of food and discovered Rita had apparently made some sort of turkey salad out of the leftovers. He made himself a couple of sandwiches and sat at the island when Bronte came into the room. "Hey you."

He glanced up to find Kelsey hovering in the doorway, looking as exhausted as he felt.

"I saw where you've had a busy day. It's all over the news."

"Don't know how he kept it up but that old man wore me out." It was true. He wasn't sure how JT had held up as long as he had, but JT had proved just how tenacious and stubborn he could be, not stopping until everyone had a full stomach, a warm bed, and in some cases, some cash to keep them going.

"Well, on top of the good you did, maybe someone will see you because of the exposure and come forward. Help you remember."

Was she hoping that was the case? To be rid of him?

Maybe it was because he was tired and hungry and frustrated with his lack of memories, but her words rubbed him the wrong way. "Maybe. The sooner the better, right?"

"Devon, I didn't mean it like that."

He picked up the sandwiches to take with him and stood. "Goodnight, Kelsey."

❄

The following evening Devon stopped in his tracks and stared at Kelsey from across the crowded ballroom.

He'd caught a glimpse of her red dress just before the penthouse elevator doors had closed on her and the doc, but that glimpse had been nothing compared to seeing her now.

Red dress, red lips. Those eyes. The other women in the room just didn't compare.

"Quite the sight, isn't she?"

JT's voice rang with pride and Devon nodded. "That she is."

"You know, son, if you took a liking to Kelsey, you'd have my blessing."

Devon turned and met JT's gaze. "That would be unprofessional."

"Bah, boy. I'm not a fool. I see how you two look at each other."

"She's a beautiful woman--with a boyfriend."

"Neil? No. He just caught her at a weak moment is all. She knows better than to trust him again."

"That's not what you said the other day. Besides, looking at them, I'm not so sure about that." From the look of things she and the doc were back together or else well on their way.

"Did I miss something?"

Devon wished he'd kept the comment to himself. "Nothing important."

"Now don't give me that, son. What's got you looking like a kid who dropped his candy?"

"The doc insinuated to Kelsey that my memory loss might not be real."

"What? Never did like a man who disparaged another's character. But what's the problem?"

"The problem is that she's worried it's true."

"She told you that?"

"She didn't have to." He and Kelsey had had a great evening the night they'd skated and walked the city streets. But the issues she'd had in the past with people befriending her only because of JT's wealth had taken their toll and instilled a distrust he didn't know how to overcome. Add in her ex's remarks and Kelsey was wary and justifiably so.

Or maybe... the bodyguard wasn't good enough for the heiress?

His gut told him that wasn't true but how was he to know when he barely knew her? Whatever he felt for her had formed quickly, since waking up in the hospital. Only a fool would think himself in love in that short span of time. How could he be in love when he didn't remember his own name?

"You're catching quite a few glances from the ladies. Go talk to them. Make Kelsey jealous. My Celia never did like it when other ladies made eyes at me and I'd bet my boots Kelsey won't like it either."

Devon glanced pointedly at JT's feet. "You aren't wearing boots."

"Are you really going to give up that easily? I'm never wrong about people but you're making me doubt myself, son. I believed you to be a fighter."

Devon was getting tired of the old man badgering

him. "I almost kissed her, JT. Several times. Is that what you want to hear?"

"Why didn't you?"

"Because I don't know who I *am*. And in this case, *almost* is as good as it can get until I do. After that day with Kelsey... I dreamed about another woman."

"What woman?"

"I don't *know*."

"Then it could be anyone. Maybe a sister."

"You don't kiss a sister the way I kissed this woman." He raised an eyebrow in JT's direction. "Still want me going after Kelsey when I could be involved with someone I don't remember?"

JT scratched his face before smoothing a hand down the front of his tuxedo. "Well, now, that does throw a kink in the plans."

"What plans?"

"Oh, nothing. Just an old man's wishful thinking. Have you told Kelsey about this dream of yours?"

"No. She brought up the question of whether my memory loss is real and there wasn't a need. Besides, she's avoided me since and... she is here with him."

"You know it could be nothing. Almost kissing Kelsey could've brought up a memory about an old girl-friend. Ever consider that?"

Was that possible?

"Have you talked to Kelsey tonight? Told her she's pretty?"

"No. She was already on the elevator with the doc. You know, her date."

"You can still tell her she's pretty. I'll do you a solid, son. I'll go get her to dance and you come over in a minute and cut in."

"What? No. JT--"

The elderly man walked off despite Devon's protests and Devon watched while JT extracted Kelsey from the group where she stood beside the doc and led her onto the dance floor.

After a couple of slow spins JT looked at Devon and motioned for him. Devon growled under his breath. He wanted to ignore JT and pretend he hadn't seen the man's wave but who knew what JT might do next.

Unpredictable topped JT's list of characteristics.

Several long strides carried Devon onto the dance floor. JT turned Kelsey once more, timing the turn with Devon's arrival.

"There you are. Kelsey, Devon has something he wants to tell you."

"What?"

Kelsey's expression revealed her surprise, quickly followed by wariness as she realized she'd been set up.

"You two dance. I'm going to go sit with the old people until dinner is served."

JT held her hand out for Devon to accept and Kelsey slowly moved into his arms to resume dancing. "I'm sorry about that. Your grandfather is a little..."

"Pushy? Don't worry about it. I should be the one apologizing to you. You, um, wanted to talk to me?"

"You look beautiful."

She smiled at the compliment.

"Thank you. You clean up pretty well yourself. What was it you wanted to tell me?"

Devon couldn't stop the smile that fought to form. "That you look beautiful," he told her again.

"Oh."

"You and the doc..."

Kelsey lifted her chin and met his gaze and those eyes of hers stared into his soul. "Is that a question?"

"I suppose it is."

"We're not back together."

"So you've been avoiding me because of what the doc said?"

A flush rose from her chest all the way into her face.

"Then let me set the record straight. Kelsey, my memory loss is real and after we almost kissed... I dreamed about kissing another woman."

"*Oh,* I see."

"No, you don't. Kelsey, I want to kiss you. To *date* you," he added, staring into her eyes, hoping she could see the truth in his words. "But not until my memory returns and I know who I am. More than anything, I need you know I'm not pretending. I'm not trying to con you. Can you... trust me?"

Chapter 31

Devon's words stayed with Kelsey all through dinner, the presentation of awards, and the silent auction that evening.

She left Neil talking to a colleague and moved on to peruse the auction items. When she looked up after completing her trip around the many tables, Neil was nowhere to be seen.

Kelsey slipped a drink from the tray of a passing server and took a sip, enjoying the beautiful dresses worn by the females in attendance. Spotting the man Neil had been talking to, she made her way over and asked if he knew Neil's whereabouts.

"I'm not sure but I think I saw him heading out to the patio."

She chatted with him a moment longer, and after not seeing JT or Devon, went on her way in search of Neil.

The outdoor patio had been decorated for the event with portable heaters and lights and brightly colored decorations.

Several couples sat near the metal heaters for warmth, a few other guests were smoking cigarettes.

She shivered from the breeze blowing in from above the building's windbreakers and was about to go back inside when she thought she spotted Neil's blond hair in a shadowy area behind one of the heaters and foliage.

Kelsey opened her mouth to call his name but something held her words inside. She quietly walked around the foliage and identified the man as Neil, arm braced against building as he courteously blocked the breeze from the woman he so passionately kissed. "Let me guess? Another set up like you claimed the last one was when you were caught like this?"

Neil's retreat could only be described as comical.

"Kelsey..."

Neil looked from her to the girl then back at her and Kelsey couldn't help but laugh. "Goodnight, Neil. I'll see myself home."

"Kelsey, *wait*."

She whirled back around to face him, holding up her hand to stop his progress. "Don't. Once might have been passed off as forgivable. But twice? No. You made decisions every step of the way to get here with her. And at every one of them you could've chosen to make the right one instead, but you didn't. Now, by all means, continue," she said, lifting her head. "Because we are most certainly *over*."

*D*evon walked through the large hotel's lobby several levels below, where the gala was held, after retrieving his and JT's coats. There were multiple televisions blaring in a nearby bar area talking about the superstorm heading their way. Devon slowed his steps when he saw the images of storm surge already beginning to flood certain parts of the city and shook his head, recalling the storm warnings on the news while he was hospitalized. Only the rich would hold a gala with a hurricane barreling down on them.

Back in motion, he'd spotted Kelsey ahead of him, racing for the hotel's main door. JT stood where Devon had left him and the elderly man took Kelsey into his arms and hold. Not a quick, goodbye, see-you-later hug but a longer, consoling type of embrace.

Not good.

Over Kelsey's shoulder JT motioned for Devon to hurry and he closed the distance between them in record time. "What's going on?"

"Sheldon is out front. Let's get into the car," JT ordered, urging them out of the lobby and away from prying eyes.

Outside, Sheldon opened the limo door for Kelsey to enter. Devon was next and he tossed the coats he held toward the far side of the vehicle. He miscalculated and they slid to the floor but none of that mattered when he saw Kelsey battling tears. "What happened?"

"She caught Neil kissing another woman."

JT was the last inside and sat closest to the door so that it was easier for him to get out.

Devon clenched his fists and seriously considered exiting the car to go find Neil when Kelsey grabbed hold of his arm.

"Please. Just take me home. I'm okay."

Punching the doc was more for his and JT's pleasure than hers but he nodded his agreement. The doc would be angry at getting caught yet again and looking for trouble. Devon didn't want JT to have to bail him out of jail for assault.

"We'll deal with Neil later, son."

Devon leaned forward to pick up the coats he'd tossed when a glove fell out of one of JT's pockets. He plucked it up without thought but the moment he actually looked at it, his world tilted.

The glove. His glove?

Wally.

The tunnels.

Yorkton.

"Devon? Are you all right?"

He'd pitched forward in his discovery and now he felt Kelsey's hands on him, keeping him in the seat beside of her. The dizziness finally started to fade and Devon looked at JT. "*Wally?*"

"Ah, son. It's okay."

Okay? "Who are you?"

"Devon? Are you okay? Sheldon, wait. I'll go get someone. Neil's still upstairs."

"*No.*"

The simultaneous command from both Devon and JT echoed throughout the limo's interior.

"Sheldon, take us home, please," JT said before pressing a button that lifted the divider between the front and rear of the vehicle. "Son, I can explain everything."

"Explain what? What's going on?"

"Kelsey, honey, his memory just came back."

Devon watched as Kelsey's eyes widened at first but then she shook her head.

"Is that true?"

Unable to lie to her because he'd promised he wouldn't mislead her, Devon nodded before slicing JT with a glare. "Who *are* you?" Devon repeated.

How did JT or Wally—*Wallingford*—know about Yorkton? What did Kelsey know? She'd told him the story about JT thinking Devon as an elf.

Which meant she knew too much.

"I was born in Yorkton, son. And I want to go home. I had family there. My brothers and a sister-- Are they alive? They'd be my age. George, Peter, Ira Walling?"

Walling. Walling wasn't much of a jump to Walling*ford*, but it was enough to be different and start anew.

"My sister's name is Margaret. And I want to know about Adeline Ford. Do you know her? Everyone called her Miss Addie."

Devon's mind swam with questions and some residual dizziness from the return of his memories, but as JT questioned him, images formed. The faces of the people he mentioned. He'd met Miss Addie on his first day in Yorkton. A widow, she was a member of the welcoming committee for anyone coming to Yorkton to work or traveling through the Lowlands to one of the other Klaas communities.

"Devon, son, say something. Please."

"What do you want?" He knew better than to respond to the other questions. Knew that to do so would reveal information only he and other Lowlanders should know. He'd have to get permission from the Elder Council. Go through protocol when it came to outsiders-- like JT.

"I told you. I want to go home. I want Kelsey to see

Yorkton and meet her family so she won't be alone when I die."

JT's mention of Kelsey seeing Yorkton reminded Devon of the storm gaining strength off the coast and the flooding already taking place. "They're in danger. The weather. I have to get back. Help." They'd have to evacuate. But to where? From the looks of those weather images there was nowhere to go. The entire city was about to get pummeled.

"You think I don't know what's at stake? That storm is massive and I've been praying nonstop for you to get your mind back before it hit. Now you have and you're going to listen to me. I can help you. *All* of you."

JT's boisterous tone bellowed throughout the back of the car as they moved along the city streets. "How?"

"Stop. You mean it's *real*?" Kelsey gripped Devon's arm, demanding his attention. "Seriously? Yorkton-- the underground city-- is a real place? Devon, you know what JT's talking about?"

"Now's not the time, my dear. But, yes, Kelsey, you're going to issue that apology for not believing me once we get them out of the Lowlands to the building. It's a long way from finished but it's high and dry, and can hold a lot of people."

Devon nodded, unable to do anything but accept the terms given the situation. "You used the door in the basement to gain access to the tunnels?"

"It's one of two marked entry points I've found in all the years I've been looking for them. The other one had partially collapsed and the tunnel access bricked up."

"How do I get to where I found you in the tunnels? If they're dry, it will be quicker to bring everyone that way instead moving above ground."

JT pulled out a pen and notepad from a console and drew a map of what he knew from the basement entry into the underground, and Devon mentally mapped the way from Yorkton to the building.

"There. Think that will get you back to where you need to be?"

He nodded and shook his head. "You were closer than you realized."

Sheldon made the turn into the building's garage, pulling in out of the wind and rain.

Devon pocketed the map and pulled his coat on over the tuxedo. His shiny dress shoes were about to get ruined. "Where's the key to unlock the basement entry? What's the code to get inside the room?"

"I'll do that. You need better clothes than those for what you're facing. Take the time to change and I will have the room open and door unblocked when you get back down."

Devon wanted to argue but the extra few minutes it took to change out of the tux and into shoes he could run in would be worth it.

Sheldon stopped the car and Devon opened the door, exiting for the elevator. He swiped the card JT had given him the day of their shopping trip and the elevator doors opened.

"I'm coming with you!"

He turned and found Kelsey running after him, a sight to behold given her gala gown and heels, her long legs flashing in and out of the slit in the side of her long skirt.

His distraction was to her benefit and gave her time to enter the elevator.

She shifted her arms behind her and leaned to one side.

"What are you doing?"

"Unzipping. It's 36 seconds to the penthouse and we can't spare a single one of them."

Unzipping?

Unzipping was all she did because, task done, she bent and went to work on one of the ankle buckles of her very high heels.

"Are you just going to watch?"

Swallowing hard and realizing she was right, he shucked his coat and pulled off his shoes, unfastened his tie, unable to take his gaze off of her while she rid herself of those insanely sexy heels.

The elevator landed at the penthouse and she bolted from it, giving him an equally sexy view of her bare lower back while she raced down the hall toward her bedroom.

It took him a minute to strip out of the tux and don the pants and boots he'd worn the night he'd left the Lowlands to help JT. Adding a shirt and grabbing the everyday coat Kelsey had given him that morning at the hospital, he checked his stride when he saw Kelsey waiting at the elevator, pulling on the second of shiny rubber rain boots. "Where do you think you're going?"

"I told you. I'm coming with you."

"I thought you meant to the penthouse to change."

"You thought wrong."

"Kelsey, it's too dangerous." He followed her onto the elevator, wondering how she managed to look so beautiful and so fierce at the same time.

"You just told me Santa's workshop is real and about

to be obliterated. Before that happens, I want to see it. It may be my only chance.'

"It's too dangerous."

"You're going."

"It's my duty."

"Mine too. According to JT I have family there and they need help."

"Kelsey--"

She planted her hands on her hips and glared at him. "One way or the other, I'm going. I'll be a lot less hassle if you let me go with you than you having to come back for me because I've gotten lost trying to follow you."

The elevator dinged and the doors opened and even though it was a horrible idea, he didn't have time to try to change her mind. "Keep up."

Chapter 32

Kelsey had never been underground. Well, *this* kind of underground. She'd ridden the subways, of course, but this was so far beyond that.

JT had supplied her and Devon with flashlights and they raced through the tunnel connected to her bookstore—her bookstore!—and followed JT's map to get them to the tunnel Devon knew would take them to Yorkton. All she could think about was the difference between the gala earlier, with people in glittering evening gowns, tuxedos, and chandeliers to the dark, dank and yes, creepy, tunnels they traversed.

Had anyone told her she'd voluntarily go underground for any reason she would've called them crazy. Now crazy meant not trusting her gut and Devon and seeing Yorkton for herself.

Devon paused in his rapid jog to look at the map and she bent double with her hands on her knees to catch her breath. She really had to work on her endurance.

"Almost there. You okay?"

She nodded. "Just waiting on you."

Devon's husky chuckle filled her ears and off they went again.

It wasn't far. Devon pointed out the area where he'd typically found JT, but only because JT had made it close to one of the cross tunnels. Devon opened a nearly invisible door in the tunnel wall and ushered her through, shutting it behind them. From there, they ran the length and entered another. And then the last door.

"The guards aren't at their stations."

She wasn't sure what that meant but given Devon's tone of voice it was bad.

He stopped at yet another door and this time Kelsey leaned against the tunnel wall, thankful for the rain gear she wore because it protected her from a hundred or so years of yuck. But in the two seconds she'd had to decide what to wear she'd guessed water resistant was best, especially underground.

"Through here."

Devon turned the wheel of a door similar to those on submarines she'd seen depicted in movies and the moment he did light filled the tunnel. Daylight. What on earth?

"Welcome to Yorkton."

Kelsey knew she stood there in open-mouthed shock and even though she wasn't sure what to expect, this wasn't it. It was an actual city albeit a small one. Two story buildings were the norm, and looked like something out of a Dickens' story. Wooden signs hung outside of a few shops, and there were trees, actual trees, and flowers. Sunlight! Las Vegas casinos had nothing on Yorkton's interior. "It's *amazing*."

"Come on. We have to find the Elder Council and Phineas Klaus."

"Klaus? As in Sinter Klaus? *Santa?*"

Devon grinned at her expression and shock but she didn't care.

"He's just a person, carrying on a long-standing family tradition."

She sucked in a sharp breath.

"What?"

"You really *are* an elf."

Devon narrowed his gaze on her. "For future reference, I really do not like being called that. Let's go."

The people they met gave her second and third glances as they passed by but seeing as how she was with Devon, or maybe because of the impending impact of the superstorm, they went on their way without comment.

They hurried down one of the city streets, passed by old-fashioned lanterns with massive hanging pots filled with greenery and decorative bulbs. Store windows were decorated for Christmas and displayed toys and clothes. Even the latest books! "How?"

"We have a long-standing network to get goods in and out. Several of the presidents have visited us in order to avoid imminent threats aboveground.

She shook her head. "*They* know?"

Devon laughed. "Of course they know."

Up ahead of them a crowd had gathered outside one of the buildings. People held bags and suitcases but just stood they're talking to one another.

Devon took her hand in his and moved toward the group and one of the men standing with his back to the entrance stiffened when he saw them.

"Where have you been?" the man asked.

"It's a long story. I need to see them."

"They're a little busy at the moment. Who is she?"

"Someone who can save us all." He tugged Kelsey forward. "Kelsey Richards," he said. "This is your uncle, Peter Walling."

Kelsey stared at the man, wishing Devon had maybe given her some sort of warning he was about to introduce her to her long-lost family.

Peter tilted his head to one side, his dark eyebrows pulling low over his eyes. "What's this?"

"I'll explain—inside. Pete, we have to get in there and talk to the Elder Council. *Now*."

Kelsey stared at the man in front of them, aware of the whispers behind them as those close enough to hear Devon's introduction spread the word.

Peter turned and opened the door, ushering Devon and Kelsey inside.

Once again, she wasn't sure what to expect but the inside of the building held an old world quality with its massive, hand-carved wooden beams towering above their heads.

Peter led the way through the throng of people standing shoulder to shoulder. With so many crowded into the room, she couldn't see into the room, only what was above.

Whispers began when the people saw them making their way through, and the deeper, masculine-voiced conversation taking place somewhere stopped.

"What's the meaning of this interruption? Has there been a change?"

Devon used his hold on her hand to tug her to his side. Down several steps in the center of what she equated to be a Town Hall, was a round table with men and women seated around it.

"My apology for the interruption, Elders," Peter said, "but Devon Sage has returned and brings news."

Kelsey glanced at Devon, only then learning his real last name.

"We have more pressing matters at hand."

"It's about the superstorm," Devon said. "And evacuating everyone to safety without revealing ourselves."

Devon had their full attention now. And so did she.

"Who are you?"

The question was directed entirely toward Kelsey. "I'm Kelsey Richards…uh, Walling."

Gasps filled the room and one of the men at the table stood slowly, his gaze narrowed on her. "M-many of you may remember my grandfather, James Taylor Walling. He was born here. He goes by JT Wallingford now. He changed his name, I suspect, to protect you all in some way. He wants to help you."

"Deputy Sage, what is the meaning of this? How do you know this Highlander?"

Devon quickly explained how he'd suffered an injury resulting in memory loss. Kelsey saw anger on many of their faces that Devon had dared to help JT and now brought an outsider to them.

"Disciplinary action will be taken at a later time."

"Yes, sir."

"What? No. How can you discipline him for saving a man's life?"

"Kelsey, hush," Devon ordered.

"Your grandfather's life wouldn't have been in danger had he not tried to break the covenant he'd agreed to when he chose to leave us."

"He's *dying*." The words came out of her mouth before she could stop them and she swayed on her feet from simply saying them aloud.

Devon's arm slipped around her shoulders to steady her and she was grateful for his strength to lean on.

The man who'd stood from the table upon hearing her name moved closer to them, his gaze locked on Kelsey's the entire time.

"H-he has a medical condition and wants to make amends. To right the wrongs he's done, he says. It's his last wish. Please. Don't deny him."

"She looks just like our mother, Georgette. Spitting image of her at the same age."

Kelsey battled tears as she held the man's gaze, only then understanding JT's need for her to connect with their family. To have someone else on this earth bonded by blood. "You l-look like him."

"Come here, child."

The man opened his arms and without conscious thought Kelsey moved down a half dozen stairs and threw herself against the other version of JT.

The man kissed the top of her head and squeezed her tight.

"I'm George," he said. "Your grandfather's younger brother by eight years."

When he released her, an older woman stood nearby and took his place.

"I'm Margaret," she said. "James Tyler's sister." When she released Kelsey, she motioned for two men to come to them. "My sons, your cousins-- James and Tyler."

These men were in their mid to late fifties and had the same look and build as JT.

"This is not the time for a family reunion."

"Actually, it is," Kelsey stated, drawing a few eyebrow raises from those near her. "JT sent us because he--*we*--want to help." She squeezed Margaret's hand "You're family and he's been desperate to find you again. And now with the superstorm-- No one has ever seen anything like it. You *have* to leave Yorkton. I know you don't want to risk exposure, but Devon is right—there's a way for you to leave without anyone—any more High-landers—becoming the wiser, but it has to be now, before the tunnels fill with storm surge. Devon and I can show you the way to JT's building. It's thirty stories and *empty*, and will get you out of danger."

The men remaining around the table bent their heads and whispered to one another and as far as Kelsey was concerned they wasted too many valuable seconds deciding the inevitable.

"How much time do we have before the tunnels are impassible?"

"Water is already trickling in from above due to the outer bands of the hurricane," Devon informed them.

"Sir, storm surge is already flooding lower areas. We estimate it will begin here within the hour," Peter stated.

"We knew this day might come. Yorkton has been blessed with nearly a hundred years of safety and secu-rity but God has other plans for us now. Issue a manda-tory evacuation order," the man said to Peter. "Lowlanders have ten minutes to gather what belongings they can carry for escape through the tunnels. Deputy Sage, you and Kelsey will lead the way."

The meeting disbanded quickly with no one sticking around to dawdle. A siren sounded, followed by an announcement that was broadcast throughout the city.

Kelsey stood on the steps of the building where the meeting had taken place and watched as the small city assembled itself like soldiers going off to war. And so they were. Short of a miracle, their home would never be the same. The life they'd known...

"Kelsey, stay close."

She'd left the steps but turned at the sound of Devon's call, nodding. She had a matter of minutes to see everything. Precious minutes JT would never have.

She took out her cell phone and began snapping photos, just to give JT an image to hold onto. The beautiful brick under her feet, the store windows. His sister Margaret talking to someone as she cradled a baby in her arms. The "sky" overhead looking so bright and blue. Bikes lined up at a stand.

There was a fountain and cafe at the end of one street, and as she ran to the next she saw gardens, a grocery, a doctor's office, and school with the sweetest little pictures in the windows.

The lights flickered and the city flashed dark. Women and children screamed and shouts were heard.

"Kelsey!"

She retraced her steps and was met by Devon who looked a bit frantic. "You were to stay put."

"I want to see it. For JT," she said, holding the phone out to show him.

The lights flickered on again but now the interior of Yorkton seemed dimmer.

"There's no time, Kelsey. I'm sorry."

She and Devon led the way through the tunnels but it took five times as long to get through them because of the sheer number of people. Young and old, with the sick and elderly needing to be carried or wheeled along.

Children whose little legs couldn't carry them very fast but their parents' arms were full of younger ones. The group reminded Kelsey of television images, refugees fleeing danger with only their most prized possessions. Looking wild-eyed and scared and traumatized by sheer fear.

The storm surge began with an inch or so of water simply appearing out of nowhere. That inch quickly turned into a foot by the time they made it to the building's basement entry.

But they'd made it and she and Devon both breathed easier because of it.

Kelsey and JT quickly set to work loading the elevators with some of the five hundred or so people to send them on their way to the safety of the above floors with light and heat. While JT handled those above, Kelsey stayed downstairs at the elevator and continued the task for those unable to take the stairs, anxiously waiting for Devon to appear in the narrow basement entry.

Several hours after leading the evacuation through the tunnels, Devon and Peter entered JT's building and closed the door behind them. Devon found Kelsey waiting for him. "You should've gone upstairs."

Kelsey shook her head. "Not without you."

Devon ushered Kelsey onto the elevator, holding her close to his side. She looked completely exhausted, no doubt worn out from the stress and events of the night —now wee hours of the morning.

The group rode upward in silence, another indication of their fatigue.

The elevator dinged and Kelsey straightened to get off but Devon snagged her arm. "I'll see Kelsey upstairs and return in a few minutes to see if anyone needs anything."

The men exited and Devon pressed the code for the penthouse.

"I'm okay. I can't go to the penthouse when I need to be there to help."

"It's been a long night. Everyone is resting. There's nothing you can do that can't wait until tomorrow, but I'll check one last time before I turn in. You need to sleep before you collapse. And I need to do this."

Devon pressed her back against the wall and palmed her jaw, tilting her head up for the kiss he'd wanted nearly since the first moment he'd laid eyes on her but didn't know if he was free to take.

But now he knew.

She tasted like the champagne and chocolate served at the gala, smelled like the rain outside mixed with soft skin and whatever she'd sprayed on her hair.

Felt soft and curvy and like his every wish.

By the time he realized the elevator doors had opened and ended the kiss, Kelsey looked more than pleasantly dazed. So he kissed her again. Because he couldn't help himself.

"I take it you're not married," she whispered with a tired smile teasing her lips.

He kissed her again, lingering over the act, and smiling all the while. "No. My name's Devon Sage."

Kelsey wrapped her arms around his neck and used

her hold to kiss him again. "It's a pleasure to finally meet you, Mr. Sage."

Chapter 33

---

*S*pring...

*S*Yorkton was completely destroyed by the massive storm surge and late season hurricane that ravaged the east coast. It took weeks for the water to fully recede, months for the destruction to be fully assessed and the final decision made not to return to the Lowlands.

But in the aftermath of that devastation *New Yorkton* formed. Because of JT's generosity and help in time of desperate need, the Elder Council decided to review their laws regarding outsiders, like their Alaskan counterparts had. Kelsey was inordinately grateful, since it meant she and JT were welcomed into the fold.

"Are you ready, Mrs. Sage?" Amanda asked.

Kelsey took a breath and slowly released it. She was more than ready to go back to her husband and the celebration of their special day after a quick trip to the bathroom that every bride knew required more than one set of hands in order to manage skirts and veils and heels.

She walked to the door beside Amanda and spotted JT across the crowded rooftop looking spiffy in his tux and top hat. "The cane might be a little over the top but it suits him, doesn't it?"

Amanda lifted her bouquet to hide her grin.

"Shall we dance?"

Devon came to her and held out his hand, led her to the dance floor. The rooftop looked amazing with its flowers and fountains and gauzy drapes blowing in the breeze as the sun set in the distance, but she only had eyes for Devon.

"Keep looking at me like that and we may have to sneak away."

"Okay."

He lowered his head and nipped her lips, a masculine sound emerging from him that made her heart race with pleasure.

The last six months may have started on a sad note but here, now, everything was perfect and right in the world. It had taken some doing, but New Yorkton was back to performing its duties for the greater good of the world, helping, serving those in need, and doing all of those things that fell under the umbrella of the "magic of Christmas" with even more efficiency.

"Look," Devon whispered, shifting his head to toward the right.

She turned her head to where Devon indicated and saw JT leading Ms. Addie onto the dance floor. The woman beamed with pleasure and love, and Kelsey wouldn't be at all surprised if there was a second wedding very soon. JT and Ms. Addie might be up there in age but what did that matter when it came to love and honoring it as the most precious of gifts?

Later that evening, after they said their goodbyes to their guests, Devon caught her hand and lifted it to his lips. "Ready for your surprise?"

Seeing as how it was now officially their honeymoon she grinned. "Are you finally going to tell me where we're going?"

"You'll see... eventually."

They entered the elevator and Devon pressed the buttons before taking her into his arms and kissing her, not stopping until the elevator dinged.

"Close your eyes."

"What?"

"Close your eyes. And no peeking."

Kelsey did as ordered and allowed Devon to lead her off the elevator, one sniff alerting her to the fact they were in her bookstore. Any booklover knew the smell of books.

"Open."

The decorating had been continued here. There were lights draped from bookshelves, flowers. A beautifully appointed bed that looked like something from a fairytale. Champagne.

"It's just for the night. Since we timed the ceremony for sunset, I thought maybe instead of a hotel or the penthouse before our flight tomorrow, we'd stay here and have a do-over of your favorite sleepover."

He ran a finger down her back and she shivered in pleasure.

"Do you like it?"

She shook her head, wondering how on earth something as awful as a gunshot wound and JT's crazy talk could have led her to this day, this moment. This man. "It's perfect, Devon. Just…perfect." She leaned into him for balance and tugged his head low for another kiss. "I'm so glad you turned out to be *my* secret Santa."

Devon kissed her again. And again.

"I'm glad you made our first Christmas together a Christmas to remember."

I HOPE YOU ENJOYED SECRET SANTA 2: A CHRISTMAS TO REMEMBER! BE SURE TO CHECK OUT Secret Santa **FOR ANOTHER WONDERFUL HOLIDAY READ, OR MORE OF KAY'S BOOKS WHEREVER BOOKS ARE SOLD.**

Book List

MONTANA SECRETS SERIES:

- HEALING HER COWBOY
- IT HAD TO BE YOU
- HERS TO KEEP
- MILLION DOLLAR STANDOFF
- HIS CHRISTMAS WISH
- THEIR SECRET SON

THE SEASIDE SISTERS SERIES:

- THE LAST GOODBYE
- LATTES AND LULLABYES
- MAP OF DREAMS
- WORTH THE RISK
- LOST LOVE FOUND

TAMING THE TULANES SERIES:

- SMALL TOWN SCANDAL
- THEIR SECRET BARGAIN
- CROSSING THE LINE
- THE NANNY'S SECRET
- SOMEONE TO TRUST

THE STONE RIVER SERIES:

- WORTH THE WAIT
- NOT BY SIGHT
- THROUGH THE VALLEY (Retitled to MORE THAN LOVE)

- LEAD ME NOT (Retitled to TO PROTECT HER)
- CHRISTMAS AT HOLLY WOOD
- THEIR CHRISTMAS MIRACLE
- SECOND CHANCES

SMALL TOWN SCANDALS SERIES:

- BRODY'S REDEMPTION
- FALLING FOR HER BOSS
- WITH THIS MAN

SECRET SANTA SERIES:

- SECRET SANTA
- SECRET SANTA II: A CHRISTMAS TO REMEMBER

MAKE ME A MATCH SERIES:

- ROMANCE RESET
- RULES OF ENGAGEMENT
- THE MATCHMAKER'S SECRET
- PERFECTLY MISMATCHED
- BY THE BOOK

CAROLINA COVE SERIES:

- SEASCAPES AND VEGAS MISTAKES
- SEASHELLS AND WEDDING BELLS
- SEA GLASS AND SECOND CHANCES
- SEA BLUE AND LOVING YOU
- SEA VIEW AND SOMETHING NEW

COMING SOON: (LINKS WILL BE UPDATED ASAP)

THE BLACKWELL BROTHERS SERIES:

- BABY BE MINE
- SECOND CHANCE WEDDING
- THE GETAWAY GUY
- OFF-LIMITS LOVE
- FLIRTING WITH FOREVER

SIGN UP FOR KAY'S NEWSLETTER AND RECEIVE UPDATES ON NEW RELEASES, CONTESTS, AND PRE-RELEASE BOOK INFORMATION.

About the Author

Kay Lyons always wanted to be a writer, ever since the age of seven or eight when she copied the pictures out of a Charlie Brown book and rewrote the story because she didn't like the plot. Through the years her stories have changed but one characteristic stayed true— they were all romances. Each and every one of her manuscripts included a love story.

Published in 2005 with Harlequin Enterprises, Kay's first release was a national bestseller. Kay has also been a HOLT Medallion, Book Buyers Best and RITA Award nominee. Look for her most recent novels with Kindred Spirits Publishing.

For more information regarding her work, please visit Kay at the following:

www.kaylyonsauthor.com

@KayLyonsAuthor (Twitter)

Kay Lyons Author (Facebook)

Author_Kay_Lyons (Instagram)

Kay Lyons, Author (Pinterest)

SIGN UP FOR KAY'S NEWSLETTER AND RECEIVE UPDATES ON NEW RELEASES, CONTESTS, PRE-RELEASE BOOK INFORMATION, EXCLUSIVES AND MORE!